CHAMELEONS AND A CORPSE

MADIGAN AMOS ZOO MYSTERIES

RUBY LOREN

BRITISH AUTHOR

Please note, this book is written in British English and contains British spellings.

PROLOGUE

The last conversation I ever had with Timmy Marsden was not a happy one. In the three months since our brief holiday to Mallorca, I'd got to know the man on the other end of the phone quite well, so it wasn't actually a huge surprise that he was about to make trouble for my fiancé.

It was only fairly recently that Auryn had been back in touch with Timmy. As the Avery family hadn't been short of money when Auryn was younger (or had at least wanted it to look that way) he'd been packed off to the local private school until he'd been old enough to duck out at sixteen in order to take on various business courses, which had eventually lead to him wrangling a zookeeper apprenticeship from his father.

My own education had been provided courtesy of the free primary and secondary school local to where I'd lived growing up, so it was strange to me to learn that Auryn's old classmates were still important to him when I'd never been close to mine. When I'd queried why he'd never mentioned them before, Auryn had explained that even before his father

1

had been caught for his crimes, it had been known in certain circles that the zoo was failing - and Erin Avery had not been a well-liked man. This shunning had been passed on to Auryn and apparently it was only now that the zoo was succeeding and Auryn had been deemed respectable that his old 'friends' were coming out of the woodwork.

Timmy Marsden was one of this group. In some ways, he had more in common with Auryn than the other fair-weather friends. He too had been kept under scrutiny by the elite community. I privately agreed that Timmy's scrutiny was largely well-deserved. When I'd attended a summer barbecue thrown by him and his wife, Scarlett, I'd heard more than enough tales about Timmy's antics to form my own opinion. When I'd reminded myself that it wasn't fair to judge on hearsay, Timmy himself had filled in the blanks by downing an entire bowl of punch. According to the stories, this was the all-new down-to-earth Timmy. I was glad I hadn't seen him at his 'peak'.

This was the reason why Timmy had been overlooked for entry into the pretentiously named club, The Lords of the Downs, until now... and he seemed determined to muck it up.

"I'm going to be a tad late. Something's come up. You go on with Auryn and Jon. I'll be there soon," Timmy said in his usual lackadaisical manner when I answered the phone. I'd continued trying to pat my hair into place whilst I listened to this non-excuse of an excuse but now I gave up. My hair wasn't going to get any tamer and I still had to make some kind of attempt at makeup. A phone call from Timmy wasn't going to make that any more likely to happen, but I'd answered Auryn's phone because he was struggling to get his bow tie right in the bathroom.

"Is everything okay?" I asked, torn between exasperation at my own appearance and Timmy's far too relaxed attitude.

"Is it Rameses?" I'd met Timmy's prized Pharaoh Hound, Rameses, at the barbecue.

"No, he's fine," Timmy replied, sounding annoyingly distracted from our conversation. "Just pop along with the boys. Tell Jon to be a gent and not do anything I wouldn't do." He chortled a little. I reflected that that probably wasn't saying much.

"You do know how important this is, don't you?" I said, hissing a little as I tried to keep my reprimand from reaching Auryn's ears. He didn't need any additional stress today.

Honestly, I couldn't believe I was defending this ridiculous club. If someone were to ask me to come up with the most repugnant idea for a club I could, the concept behind The Lords of the Downs would only be exceeded by a group that advocated violence and hate. As it stood, The Lords of the Downs trod a very fine line in my view. For one, they only let men join. You had to be inducted before you were thirty five, or not at all, and you either had to be outstanding in your field or be some kind of legacy. To my knowledge, most of the members were legacies. And finally, someone had to die or be removed (a fate worse than death?) in order for you to join. A club made up of rich men who met up and talked about who knew what... it was everything the world feared.

When Auryn had been extended the invitation to visit a couple of meetings and subsequently be inducted into the club, I'd definitely questioned it. Surely in this modern day and age a secretive gentlemen-only society belonged in the history books? But Auryn had explained that it wasn't an invitation you turned down lightly. The members of The Lords of the Downs had a tremendous amount of influence in the local community. It wasn't in the rulebook or anything, but Auryn had definitely implied that it was this group of mysterious men who decided whether or not to favour one business over another... and that in turn could dictate the success of said business. When I'd protested that it was hardly fair that only men were allowed in the club when women owned local businesses, too (I'd been thinking about my zoo when I'd said it) he'd told me that it made it even more important for him to join - so he could represent us both. When I'd done some more complaining over exactly what I thought about that, he'd promised to tell me everything that transpired at the meetings. There was no Official Secrets Act to circumnavigate here.

Anyway, today I would get to see what it was all about for myself. It was Auryn and Timmy's induction into the club, and for that special meeting, they were each allowed to bring along a guest of their choice. Timmy had left it too late to RSVP, as was apparently his custom, so was coming alone. *Or not at all,* I silently amended.

I suddenly realised that Timmy had said something while I'd been drifting. "Sorry, what was that?"

"Oh, nothing," Timmy replied. "I promise I'll be there in a jiffy. Tell Auryn and Jon to be sure to uphold all of our Harvington House ideals."

"Wait... what are you wearing?" I asked and then blushed to my roots. I was exceedingly glad that Auryn was in the bathroom and that no one else was present. It was a sure sign that Timmy was currently distracted by something when he didn't seize on the easy joke.

"Suit trousers, a black shirt, and a blazer that matches the trousers. Also, sequin shoes," he tacked on at the last moment.

"Sequin shoes?"

"No - although I bet you'd love to see me in a pair of them, wouldn't you?" Even over the phone, Timmy Marsden was a moron.

I gritted my teeth and lamented the already long day I'd

had. One of the keepers at The Lucky Zoo was off sick, so I'd been up since six, feeding animals and doing chores. Later, I would figure that this phone call had probably taken place at around eleven o'clock, because Auryn and I were so close to leaving.

"I'm wearing brogues. Normal shoes," Timmy clarified when I didn't answer.

"Good." I'd known Auryn had been worried about what Timmy might wear to their induction. His normal fashion sense was fairly variable. He'd been wearing pink and blue golf shorts at the barbecue. All of the other men had worn linen.

My heart sank when I considered that attire wasn't going to be the biggest barrier to Timmy's frictionless induction.

"How late will you be?" I wheedled.

"Oh, a few minutes. I'll be there, don't you worry," he said, and I decided he meant it. It was clear that Timmy was distracted. I had visions of burst water pipes or small fires starting, but who really knew with Timmy? He was the sort of person who believed the world revolved around him. Everyone else could just dance to his rhythm, and there wasn't a lot that could be done to change that. After all, Timmy was getting into The Lords of the Downs by the skin of his teeth. Auryn had told me that a mob boss, who'd almost certainly committed murder by proxy, had been let in, (the key to his admission was simply that he'd avoided conviction) so for Timmy to be a tough choice was really saying something.

"Fine. See you there," I said and hung up, figuring it was best to leave Timmy to whatever was more important than joining The Lords of the Downs. It was only for Auryn's sake that I cared. New members were supposed to vouch for each other.

I returned to the impossible task of fixing makeup onto

my face and took a moment to reflect back upon what a makeup artist had once told me were my colours. I had believed that the information would go in one ear and out the other, but some of it must have stuck. I reached for my eyeshadow and added a subtle pop of green to my eyelids. *Is it too much?* I wondered. And then - to my horror - I wondered if it was too young for me. "Whoa now, you're not old!" I told myself very firmly. I had a birthday coming up and I very definitely felt that I was on the wrong side of twenty-five these days. Part of it was due to Auryn barely being in his twenties, I shook my head and went back to my mascara. I was in my twenties, too. I'd been over this too many times in my head already. It was silly to worry about it forever.

As I moved onto the fancy matte lipgloss Tiff had bought me for Christmas, I thought some more about Auryn's old school friends, Timmy and Jon. Timmy was only a few years older than Auryn, but Jon Walker-Reed was closer to my age. According to Auryn, there'd been a wide range of ages at the school and they'd surprisingly mixed. The younger boys had tended to be coerced into doing the bidding of the older group, but Auryn had informed me, rather proudly, that he'd won their respect at an early age. When I'd seen the sideways smile on Auryn's face, I'd decided I didn't want to know.

I frowned briefly at my reflection in the mirror. Jon would be here soon to pick us up. The club was meeting in a stately home belonging to their leader - whomever that may be. Only confirmed members were trusted with the location of each meeting, which was why Jon was going to be taking us. I spared a thought to wonder what Timmy would do, and then decided it wasn't my problem. Jon could send him a text, or something.

Strange as it may sound, if I had to choose my favourite from Jon and Timmy, I would have chosen Timmy. Jon was a gentleman in all respects. He was always polite and proper and dressed well. Unfortunately, he was also completely boring. Married with two kids and a wife, who was far more interesting, who enjoyed staying at home and looking after the children, there was absolutely nothing remarkable about him. After meeting him a few times, prior to Auryn's invitation to the club, and then at the barbecue, and again at Auryn's trial meeting, I'd actually begun fantasising that there had to be something more to Jon. Was he leading a double life? Did he secretly dress up in a superhero costume and exact vigilante justice on non-law abiding locals? Unfortunately, I suspected that if you scratched beneath the surface of Jon, you'd just find more boring beneath.

By comparison, Timmy had a reputation for being wild and self important, but he was also an adventurer and somehow very likeable. He was a risk taker and a man I normally would not have been adverse to Auryn and me finding friendship in. However, it had been all too clear at the barbecue that Timmy and his wife, Scarlett, had surely boarded a runaway train on the route to divorce. There'd practically been frost forming on the punchbowl between them. For that reason, I thought it would be wiser to give Timmy and Scarlett their space, rather than become embroiled in their love's demise.

I'd thought that divorce was the worst thing on the cards for Timmy's future - that and the ever-present possibility he may one day fall off the side of one of the mountains he enjoyed climbing - but fate had something far worse in store for him.

THE SECRET SOCIETY

Timmy never turned up to the club meeting. I had to endure an entire hour and a half of sitting next to a silently furious Auryn. They were supposed to have vouched for each other and it didn't exactly look good for Auryn that the man he was supposed to be vouching for, and be vouched for in return, hadn't bothered to show up. The leader of the meeting, a man named Nigel Wickington who apparently owned some huge industrial steel firm, was hardly thrilled either. All through the meeting as it became more and more apparent that Timmy wasn't going to materialise, he shot murderous looks in our direction. Even Jon had taken the first opportunity to join up with some of his other friends in the club.

As we were being shunned, I'd taken some time to look at the room we were in. It was a rather fabulous sitting room that had been set with chairs and even featured a little stage, that I assumed was only brought out for meetings. When I'd been introduced as Auryn's guest, everyone had been quick to tell me that they didn't often meet in this location. I thought the presence of the stage and the familiarity everyone seemed to have with the whereabouts of the facilities proved otherwise, but I didn't comment. The secret society could keep its secrets it if made the members happy.

"It's not a secret society," Auryn hissed in my ear.

I turned to him in surprise. "I didn't say anything!"

"You had that look on your face."

"What look?" I hissed back.

"The one where you look superior and amused at the same time - like you think this is all silly. It's probably why women aren't allowed!"

I was about to argue back when an older woman, who I assumed was Nigel's wife, or perhaps a maid (it was a big house) walked into the room pushing a tea trolley. She and I looked at one another and a knowing look passed between us.

"See!" Auryn said, folding his arms and looking annoyed. I did my best to conceal my grin. The woman pushing the tea trolley looked for all the world like a mother who entertained the flights of fancy of a group of children and their special secret club where no girls were allowed.

After tea and biscuits, Auryn was officially welcomed into The Lords of the Downs. The rest of the meeting was dedicated to business affairs, but apart from a few major bulletins, I noted that this was mostly conducted in secretive huddles, and whenever I got within earshot the whispering would die down. It was just like being back in the school playground, only, the worrying thing was, whatever these men were whispering about apparently had a lot of influence. It was clear that the men in this group were all used to being rich, and perhaps whatever was being discussed in these whispering huddles was how they stayed that way. *It's not what you know but who you know,* I thought to myself, feeling annoyed by the club all over again. I wondered if there was an equivalent women-only club where we could whisper to each other and have secret meetings without the men knowing.

I decided that we were all far too grown up for that.

Auryn reappeared with Jon from the group where they'd been chatting. I'd remained next to the tea and biscuits, having a chinwag with the lady, who was indeed the wife of Nigel Wickington. We'd been having a giggle at the men's expense when they rejoined us.

"We'll pop by Timmy's place on the way back, shall we?" Jon said. Both he and Auryn had grim expressions on their face.

"I can't believe he's done this to us. Even when he acted the goat back at school, he was never disloyal," Auryn commented.

"We'll set him straight."

I bit my lip to try to regain some semblance of serious-ness after the way I'd heard Annemarie Wickington talk about her husband's club. She'd merely confirmed my views about the puffed-up society.

Auryn shot me a withering look that probably meant my 'secret societies are stupid' expression had made a return. Before he could tell me to remove it, we were approached by one of the elder members. Jon introduced him as being Lord Something-Or-Other (not actually his name, I just hadn't listened very well.)

"What ever happened to the other chap, Timothy?" He asked it with so much politeness that it was the English equivalent of a slap in the face.

"He said something had caused him to be running a bit late. It must have turned into an emergency," I invented for all our sakes.

"Congratulations on becoming a member," the elderly lord said, inclining his head towards Auryn without acknowledging my words. The implication was clear - Auryn may be in the club for now, but he'd do well to watch who his friends were. We were all guilty by association.

It was a relief when the three of us managed to slip out of the meeting without encountering any further judgemental rich men. I shook my head and opened my mouth to say something along those lines, but Auryn shot me a sharp sideways look. He was already on thin ice here and expressing my views to Jon, a member of the group, would do him no favours. I decided that Auryn and I were going to have a serious talk about this ridiculous club later on when we had some alone time. For now, I kept quiet.

Jon started up the car and it wasn't long before we were zipping along the country lanes that connected the villages caught in orbit Gigglesfield. Timmy Marsden lived in a sizeable country house down a quiet lane next to a handful of other large houses. I knew from the barbecue that the back of the property extended out a long way before turning into fields and woodland.

"What could possibly have kept him? Timmy doesn't even lift so much as a finger around the house. He has a housekeeper who comes in every other day to do all of that stuff," Jon complained as we drew into the driveway. I noted that Timmy's navy blue BMW was still parked just inside the garage. "Auryn, can you go inside and find the devil? I need some time to cool off. Timmy has done stupid things in the past, but this trumps them all! He knew I was sticking my neck out by recommending him to the club. When his old man passed on a few years ago, he should have been invited then, but he was deemed unsuitable. Like a complete fool, I swore to the elders of the club that he'd changed his ways."

Auryn got out of the car and I followed suit. Anything was better than staying in the car with a brooding man, and I was also very curious as to what could have possibly been more important than an induction into a smug boys' club. My foot landed on something that had been left on the drive. I picked the item up and discovered it was a hand-tooled leather dog lead. With a sinking heart, I realised I recognised it. I signalled to Auryn to wait and placed the lead back in the car inside the handbag I'd brought with me. Jon looked back with curiosity. His expression closed as soon as he saw what it was, and he went back to staring at the sky through the windscreen.

I caught up with Auryn and we made it to the front door. Some sense of foreboding must have taken over Auryn, too, as instead of knocking, he reached out and gave it a push. The door swung open. We exchanged a look, both silently thinking that Timmy was probably not alone.

Various snatches of gossip at the barbecue had informed me that Timmy wasn't exactly big on fidelity. His wife, Scarlett, was apparently just as bad, if not worse, if you took what some of the barbecue lads had been saying as the honest truth. I'd taken it all with a big fat grain of salt, but if Timmy did have a lover round, it could explain why he hadn't shown up at the club.

There was the sound of clattering paws before Rameses appeared around the corner, his tail wagging back and forth like an overexcited rudder. He rushed straight up to me and thrust his head into my hands so I could pat his head. He made a lousy guard dog. Timmy had talked to me about him at the barbecue, and I'd learned that the breed had originated from Malta and were bred to hunt rabbits. But whilst Rameses had apparently cost an arm and a leg to buy, due to his rarity, he'd turned out to be more of a lapdog than a hunting hound.

"Where's your owner, hmmm? Where's Timmy?" I asked the tan dog, bending down to talk to him. I froze when I saw something dark around his mouth. Had Rameses been injured? I looked at my hand and discovered there was a big red smear across it.

"Auryn..." I held up my hand so he could see. "I don't think it's his," I said after a brief inspection of the dog. "I'll check upstairs."

"I'll look down here." Auryn's mouth was set in a grim line. "Shout if you see anything."

I walked up the stairs with Rameses on my heels. I tried not to think too hard about the red stains around his mouth and instead kept my wits about me. The unlocked door could mean an intruder and there was every possibility that someone was still in the house...

I nearly jumped out of my skin when I saw the mirror. My own scared face looked back at me. My wavy hair had puffed out a little and my cheeks were drained of colour. Although it was July and baking hot outside, I felt icy cold. But it wasn't the chill that made me look like a ghost. I couldn't shake the feeling that something dreadful had happened.

I walked into the bedroom and looked at the unmade bed. Covers were strewn around. The housekeeper clearly hadn't been by today. The door to the ensuite bathroom was open. I walked in to the lavish room and touched a finger to the bottom of the jacuzzi-style bath. It was bone dry. No one had bathed or showered in it recently. Rameses nudged against my leg, probably staining it with blood. I looked down and he whined nervously.

Then I heard Auryn calling for me. My feet felt especially heavy when I walked back down the stairs with Rameses leading the way. It was as if they didn't want to carry me to find out what it was that had made Auryn's voice sound so strange when he'd shouted my name. I steeled myself for the worst and walked into the kitchen. My eyes fell on a mug of tea that had been left out on the side. I reached out and touched the side. It was cold. With great reluctance, I turned my attention to the violent splash of red that drew the eye better than a well-thought out flower arrangement.

Timmy Marsden's body was partially concealed by the kitchen counter. He was lying on his back in a pool of blood with his feet facing the glass double doors that led out onto the long garden. A spray of red coated the side of the kitchen unit that faced the doors. Rameses pushed passed me, stepping in the crimson liquid. His paw prints showed he'd tracked through the blood once already. He scratched at the glass door, spreading the mess even further. Auryn covered his hand with his sleeve and then gingerly reached out and compressed the handle on the door furthest away from the body.

"Don't slip!" I warned when Auryn's foot got dangerously close to a patch of water on the floor. The door proved to be unlocked and swung open, letting Rameses run free to do his business.

I looked out of the open door down the garden after the disappearing dog. The sounds of a radio playing and splashing indicated that Ethan Pleasant was out in his hot tub. He'd been out in the tub on the day of the barbecue. After Timmy had good-naturedly called over the fence and asked him to turn his radio down, Auryn had told me that Ethan was something of a cyber wiz kid. He'd made a million by the time he was twenty and now that number was assuredly much, much higher. Auryn had then embarrassedly admitted his father had turned Ethan away when he'd come to the zoo to suggest a hi-tech admissions system. According to Auryn, it had been beyond his father to imagine something like that working, in spite of the money it would save long-term on staffing. My fiancé had then added that he himself wouldn't consider it because the thought of firing a group of people who'd helped the zoo to rise up out of the ashes of failure was incredibly harsh. I personally thought that when people visit a zoo, the first thing they should see is a friendly, helpful face. Sometimes there are more important things than efficiency.

In the distance, I heard a dog bark and then Rameses' response. I shook my head at the innocuous sounds and then pulled the door shut. Life continued as normal all around us, unaware that death lurked inside the house.

"We have to get out of here," Auryn mumbled.

I glanced at him and realised his face had turned the colour of curdled milk. "Come on. Let's go outside and tell Jon what's happened. Someone's got to call the police." I held a hand out and Auryn took it gratefully. I led him back through the house and out through the front door, where the smell and feeling of death faded to nothing.

"He was only a few years older than me," Auryn muttered, the horror of death touching him.

I nodded and patted his arm. I was getting to be fairly well-versed in this kind of thing.

Jon got out of the car when he saw our grim faces. "What happened? Where's Timmy?"

"Dead," Auryn managed and then went to sit in the car with his head bowed.

Jon looked at me for clarification.

I nodded. "It looks like someone killed him. I'm going to call the police."

I took out my phone and dialled the emergency number before asking for the police. Then, I recounted what I'd seen and checked the address with Jon. The rest was a blur that I answered on autopilot. When I hung up, Jon was looking from me to Auryn and had questions written all over his face.

"What happened?" he asked again.

"I think... I think someone might have stabbed him," I

managed, feeling faint all of a sudden. I took a couple of deep breaths and tried to focus. Fortunately, by the time the police arrived, I was feeling a little better. I'd seen bodies before, but this one had been really awful. *All of that blood...*

I blinked and nodded my head when the police asked to be shown the scene. This time, Jon followed me into the house - although he gasped and shrank back before turning and walking back outside as soon as Timmy's corpse came into view. I first focused on the cup of tea, never to be drunk, before my eyes shifted to the garden outside of the glass doors, so fresh and alive and unlike the death that lurked inside. I remembered letting Rameses out and moved to open the door to call him back.

"Don't!" a police officer warned and I lowered my hand an inch shy of the handle. "This is a crime scene," he reminded me.

What had I been thinking anyway? Letting Rameses back in would only cause the police more trouble, and he was probably far happier outside anyway. I was sure that someone would come to collect him later.

"You should probably go back outside. Someone will be along to take your statement. I've called for backup," the officer said in gentler tones.

I nodded, still looking out at the garden and the blue sky before tearing my eyes away and managing to not focus on the body on the floor.

Jon and Auryn were both standing by the car with Officer Miles, whom I recognised from the incident around Christmas time that had taken place at Avery Zoo. If I were being truly honest, I had hoped I wouldn't be seeing him again for a long, long time.

After we'd all briefed the officer on what we knew, we were sent along to the police station.

"I've got to call Timmy's family. They deserve to know,"

Jon said when we were sitting in the reception area of the station, waiting to be called in.

"Who's going to tell his wife?" Auryn asked.

"Heavens! Scarlett! She must still be at work! Someone should tell her right away. You know what gossip is like in this town..." Jon said, running a hand through his sparse, spiky dark hair.

"I hope she is at work, for her sake," I contributed.

Both men turned to look at me.

"Well where else would she be? It's a Sunday. She works on Sundays. Actually, I think Scarlett works all of the days," Jon supplied.

"'Works'... right." I wasn't so naive.

Right on cue, the receptionist beckoned us over. "I've just received word that officers are trying to contact a Mrs Scarlett Marsden. Do any of you have contact details for her?"

"I think I've got it here," Jon said, pulling out his phone. I silently raised an eyebrow wondering why Jon would have those details to hand. I knew he'd been friends with Timmy for a long time... but had he been even more friendly with Mrs Marsden?

"There you go... my wife wanted some of that fancy shaping underwear that Scarlett's company makes. She said she'd send us over whatever my wife wanted if I gave her a ring," Jon explained when the receptionist eyed him with the same scrutiny I'd felt.

I nearly rolled my eyes. I should have known there would be nothing salacious about Jon having Scarlett's details. With Jon, all you had to do was eliminate all of the interesting possibilities and you'd be left with the correct boring and sensible one.

"Typical Timmy. He even died in a way that attracted attention," Jon muttered, and then looked horrified he'd said it out loud.

The receptionist cleared her throat and returned his phone. "Thank you. We've already tried that number. It was listed online. I suppose none of us imagined she'd put her personal number on there, but it sounds like a personal voicemail when it goes through."

"Scarlett Marsden's work colleagues claim she left work early today," a man I'd never seen before announced, striding through the double doors that led into the main station. He had short cropped blonde hair, serious blue eyes, and a lean physique. I also didn't fail to notice that he wore a uniform which was decorated with quite a few stripes and what looked like medals.

"I'm Detective Alex Gregory. I just transferred from Brighton to take over Detective Treesden's post now that he's sought early retirement."

"Early retirement?" I enquired.

"For personal reasons." Detective Gregory threw me a long speculative look when he said it. I thought I could probably have a stab at what Treesden's personal reasons had been.

"I wonder where Scarlett could be? She's so dedicated to her work," Jon prattled on whilst Auryn and I avoided making eye contact. "Timmy was so proud of her. She had this idea and he put some money into it, and now she's worth far more than he is. Was," Jon amended, looking downcast once more. "*Suck-It-In* is everything Scarlett ever dreamed of achieving. There's no reason at all for her to have killed Timmy, if that's what you're all implying right now. She already has everything she ever wanted."

"No one is implying anything. We're hoping to contact close relatives and family of the deceased in order to inform them of what has happened. After that, we will be looking to establish whereabouts in order to ascertain if there were any witnesses to the suspected crime and to further our investigation," Detective Gregory explained in a far more reasonable manner than Treesden would have done. "If you could all come this way, we're ready to take statements."

"Oh my golly gosh!" Jon said, looking perhaps even more horrified than he had when he'd seen the body. "How could I forget? There was a contract at the house - a really important one. I was supposed to look it over as a favour to Timmy and Scarlett. Timmy was going to give it to me today. I'm a solicitor," he clarified. "It was the final draft of a merger between Suck-It-In and another fairly well-known clothing company. Her big company lawyers have already looked it over but she asked me to just give it the once over right before she made her mind up. To be honest, I think she just wanted a reason to delay. I wouldn't find anything that the kind of lawyer she can afford wouldn't have already spotted. She said it was the only signed copy and that it also contained all kinds of confidential financial information. It's really important that it's found!"

"I'll send an alert to the officers at the scene and will make a note to ask Mrs Marsden, once she has been located," the woman behind reception said.

Jon's shoulders slumped a little but I noticed there were beads of sweat on his forehead that hadn't been there before. Just what was in the mysterious contract that was important enough to cause this kind of panic? Only a few moments ago Jon had claimed that Scarlett already had everything she'd ever wanted... but the existence of this merger might hint otherwise. Jon hadn't mentioned who was taking over who, and it also seemed evident that Scarlett herself had been less than certain about making the final decision. Could Timmy's death be tied up with this mystery contract?

"Why don't we go through?" Detective Gregory prompted when the drama seemed at an end. We followed him through into the bustling office.

"You're Madigan Amos, aren't you?" The detective was still looking at me speculatively.

I wondered what exactly Treesden had told him about me. I was willing to bet it wasn't anything complimentary, and I wanted to commend Detective Gregory on keeping a straight face. "I am, yes."

"I'll start with you. Officer Ernesto and Officer Becky, please take statements from the other two witnesses," Detective Gregory said with practiced ease. I had assumed that this job warranted a promotion for the new detective. He looked to be in his mid-thirties but it was obvious he already had experience of giving orders. Perhaps he'd come from a military background, I speculated.

"Ms Amos, over here if you please." The detective sat down behind a cluttered desk. My surprise at his rather humble station must have shown. "As I already said, I'm new. Things are still being sorted out in Detective Treesden's old office." He dug beneath one of the piles of folders, causing it to teeter threateningly on the verge of collapse. I was feeling something similar myself right now.

"How are you finding it so far?" I enquired, hoping to start off on the right foot with the new detective.

"Everyone here has been very welcoming. I was warned that due to it being a more rural area, things were likely to be a lot quieter than it was at my old workplace. However, that remains to be seen..." He shot me a pointed look before shuffling the papers he'd isolated from the pile.

"What were you doing when you found Timothy Marsden?"

"It's okay! It's safe!" Jon suddenly announced, standing up from the booth he was in with another officer. There was a look of relief on his face. "I messaged my wife and she messaged back to say that Scarlett delivered the contract to my place this morning. She still has it."

"Send someone over to collect it," Detective Gregory said to a passing member of the admin team. He bobbed his head and hurried off.

The detective turned back to me with a look of exasperation just starting to take hold.

"Excuse me, Sir. Sorry... can I just..." a young woman I didn't recognise, but who wore police uniform, inserted herself between me and the detective. With a flourish, she produced an all too familiar book from behind her back. "I can't believe you're here in our station! This is beyond cool. Would you mind...?" She passed over a pen and I obligingly scribbled my name on the title page, pausing only to ask to whom I was dedicating the comic.

"Officer Gemma!" Detective Gregory burst out, saving me from needing an answer on that front. I finished writing and passed it back to her.

"Love your work," she said, flashing me a grin, before scuttling away with the heat of Detective Alex Gregory's stare chasing her. I privately hoped that she would consider my autograph worth it when she received whatever disciplinary action I could sense was going to come her way.

"How come the police officers use their first names, but they always address you using your last?" I asked. I'd wondered it for a while, and seeing how derailed we'd got, it seemed as good a time as any to ask.

"It's part of an initiative for our public interacting staff to be seen as approachable," Detective Gregory told me, far from thrilled. He left it unsaid that his last name was used because someone still needed to be an authority figure.

"You were asking what I was doing when I found Timothy Marsden," I prompted with a hopeful smile.

It wasn't returned.

I silently sighed. Treesden may be gone but I had a strong

feeling that the good first impression I'd hoped to make on Detective Alex Gregory had just taken a nosedive.

"What were you doing?" he asked when I faltered.

"I was on my way back from a meeting of The Lords of the Downs club with my fiancé Auryn and his friend, Jon."

"How long was this meeting planned for?"

"I think they meet every couple of weeks."

"You think?" The detective raised his blonde eyebrows.

"I'm not actually a member. It's a men-only club. I was only allowed in today because it was Auryn's induction. It was supposed to be Timmy's, too. Someone died to let him in," I tacked on and then wondered if I was gabbling.

The detective stopped writing what I was saying down and looked up. "Someone died?"

"The club has a fixed intake. Someone has to die, or step down, or be kicked out for someone new to get in. Auryn's father lost his place, which was why Auryn was inducted. Although, it took them a while to decide upon it."

The detective looked curious, but I wasn't going to elaborate on that. He would surely find out for himself in good time. Nothing stayed a secret for long in Gigglesfield.

"Who died to let Timothy Marsden join?"

"I have no idea," I confessed. "I knew he wasn't initially considered suitable, but I only found out today that when his father died they decided he wasn't right for the club at that time. I'm not sure if they held his place, or if he was moved down the waiting list."

"There's a waiting list?" Detective Gregory looked more bemused by the second. "Just what is this club all about?"

"I think it's quite popular," I said, answering his first question. I'd gathered that much from the talk from certain people at the barbecue about how lucky Auryn was to be a legacy and have his place honoured even after his father was given the boot. I'd definitely got the impression that there were plenty of men who hoped to get into the club, but were still waiting their turn. "As for what it's about... I'm really not sure. When I went today it was just groups of men talking about their businesses. You'll have to ask them in order to get a better idea. As a woman, I'm somehow considered unworthy," I couldn't resist sniping before biting my tongue. Now wasn't the time to let my views of the club rise to the surface. I was being interviewed as a part of what would surely turn out to be a murder investigation. Timmy Marsden hadn't just fallen and died to end up the way we'd found him.

"Where were you yesterday evening and this morning, prior to the meeting?"

"He wasn't dead yesterday evening," I automatically said.

"How do you know that?" The detective looked every bit as suspicious as Treesden had when we'd had our brushes.

"I spoke to him on the phone right before we left for the meeting. He was definitely alive then."

"What time was that?"

I thought about it. "It must have been eleven? We were really close to leaving when Timmy called. Jon was picking us up first and then we were supposed to go to collect Timmy."

"Were you able to tell where he was when he made the call?"

"I assume he was still at home. He said he was going to be a little late but not to worry. I think he did intend to come to the club. He was wearing the right clothes," I remembered.

"The right clothes?"

"I asked him what he was wearing. The club has a fairly strict dress code and dressing appropriately for the occasion wasn't one of Timmy's strengths. He said he was wearing a blazer with matching trousers and a black shirt. That's what he was dressed in when he died."

"What were you doing earlier in the morning, and could anyone verify your whereabouts?" the detective pressed.

I tried to remind myself not to take any of this personally... yet. "I was at my zoo filling in for a zookeeper who called in sick. I think I said hello to most of the staff, which at that time of the morning was probably about twenty different people."

The detective nodded and made another note. "What was your impression of the deceased? Was he well-liked?" All of a sudden, Detective Gregory seemed to laser focus on me. I realised everything else had been leading up to this - the question he was really interested in having answered.

"You're asking me if he had any enemies..." I thought for a second. "He might have had some. Timmy didn't always realise when he was taking a joke too far. Perhaps he rubbed someone up the wrong way one too many times."

"What about his wife, Scarlett? Does she have enemies?"

"I really couldn't say. I only saw her in passing at the barbecue." I hesitated and then bit my tongue as I stopped myself from over-sharing about the fight they'd clearly been embroiled in on that sunny day - the one that had set the gossipers whispering about a divorce being on the cards. Someone else could tell Detective Gregory. I'd already passed on my fair share of hearsay.

"I think the most likeable member of the Marsden family is Rameses, their dog," I said with a light smile. "At least... he's my favourite."

"They have a dog?"

"Yes. Unfortunately, he stepped all over the crime scene."

"Oh, so that's what it was. One of the officers suggested that it might show signs that he'd been dead overnight and a wild animal had somehow got in."

I shook my head at the detective. "No, Auryn let him out of the door because he needed to go outside to do his business. He covered his hand with his sleeve when he did it and tried to be careful. Has no one seen him since?"

Detective Gregory shifted in his seat, sensing my alarm. "I'll make sure it's checked. The dog's not dangerous, is it?"

"No, for all his hunting breeding, Rameses wouldn't hurt a fly." Of that, I was confident. "He just needs to be found. He's apparently quite a valuable dog and it would be terrible if someone used this opportunity to steal him from an already bereaved family. Also, I don't think he'd do too well out on his own. But hopefully he's still in the garden. There's a wire fence running along near the bottom, probably to keep him in."

The detective made a note and then called someone else over to enquire about Rameses.

"Did the deceased give any particular reason why he was going to be late to the meeting?" he asked when that had been dealt with.

"He never said. It was just that something had come up. He seemed distracted but didn't elaborate. After checking his outfit choice, I let him get on with it. There was no point in delaying him further with questions."

"Okay," Detective Gregory said, although I noticed there were frown lines deepening on his forehead.

All of a sudden a round of applause went up. I spun in my seat and observed, to my horror, that none other than Detective Treesden had entered the station.

"No need for any of that. I'm just here to collect a few things I've been informed I left behind. That's what happens when you hit retirement, your brain turns to mush." He smiled a steely smile, and to my amazement, some of the staff in the station actually chuckled. I'd never seen Detective Treesden say anything approaching humour before.

Then he saw me and his smile disappeared. "Who's dead this time?"

If it was meant as a joke, it fell catastrophically flat when Detective Gregory and I both looked grim.

"Can I have a word...?" Detective Gregory asked and together the two detectives went off to chat.

Either they didn't walk far enough or they weren't aware of the carrying acoustics in the police station because I was able to overhear almost every word.

"I see you've met our resident celebrity," Treesden began in scathing tones. We really had not got on well together... even though I'd certainly helped him solve at least two murders and several other crimes to boot. When I said I'd helped to solve the murders, I really meant by making it pretty obvious who the bad guys were when they'd tried to add me to their kill lists, but that still counted, right? I was an asset!

"She seems a bit scatterbrained. When I heard she owns a zoo, works as some kind of consultant, and wrote some comic or other I expected her to be sharp," Detective Gregory was saying.

Well, ouch. I really hadn't made the impression I'd wanted to on the new guy.

"Scatterbrained? If she's trying to give you that idea it means she's probably hiding something... like she does every time."

I very nearly stood up and marched over to find them when I heard that. I'd never knowingly lied to the local police force when being questioned! It wasn't my fault that certain things had come to light when no police presence had been around. Also, there'd been times when I hadn't been sure enough to involve the police, but when the truth had been revealed it had been a little too late...

However, Treesden's accusation had got me thinking, and I'd realised that he was technically right. There was a piece of information I was still sitting on, wasn't there? I looked across and caught Jon's eye. His interviewing officer was writing up notes so we shared a moment of silent communication. He lifted his shoulders and set them down, but there was a troubled expression on his face. I took that to mean the ball was in my court as far as making a decision went.

Treesden and Gregory returned with straight faces, as if they hadn't just dragged my name through the dirt.

"What are you up to?" Treesden barked in my face.

Much as I hated to give him the satisfaction, I'd already decided I was going to cave, as they clearly already suspected something. "It's probably nothing, but I found a dog lead on the drive when I got out of the car. I thought someone might have just dropped it there accidentally. A lot of people own dogs in the rural villages," I pointed out, fairly. "I wasn't sure if it was relevant."

"Yes you were," Treesden informed me.

I sighed and reached into my bag. My hands closed around a lead and I pulled it out. "Here you go," I said, passing across the lead. I was relieved I hadn't said what kind of dog I thought the lead was for because no one would believe that the small harness I'd just handed over was for anything larger than a Jack Russell. Of course, there was every chance that if anyone bothered to test the fibres attached to it, they'd also discover that the lead belonged to a cat, not a dog. Then I'd be in for it. But for now, my little spur of the moment deception had worked.

I wasn't even sure why I'd done it. It had only been at the last moment that I'd changed my mind and given them Lucky's lead instead.

"They'll find out," Jon said when we were outside again and

I'd filled Auryn in on what I'd found on the drive and my devious sleight of hand.

I looked across at Jon and observed that in spite of his words, he looked relieved. "I'm sure they will, but at least we won't be the ones who told them. Anyway, there could be any number of explanations..."

We all looked down at the real lead, which I'd just taken out from my handbag. It had been brought back from Nepal by Timmy, who'd then gifted it to local crime historian, Andy Wright, at the barbecue as a thank you for looking after Rameses during the time he'd been away. I'd assumed that Scarlett had been too busy to care for the dog.

"I'm sure there is a good explanation for it being there," Auryn echoed, but he looked just as troubled as I felt.

When we'd pulled up and found the front door unlocked, I knew that my first assumption had been that there was a woman in the house. Even though I hadn't known him for long, I knew that Timmy had quite the history of extra-marital affairs. Although, I'd also heard that Scarlett wasn't exactly a saint herself...

The lead's presence was troubling because of the way it had been left abandoned on the drive, as if the person doing the abandoning was sending a message to the original sender that their gift was not welcome. With Timmy's reputation, I knew we could all hazard a guess as to why that might be.

Unfortunately, Auryn worked pretty closely with Andy's wife. Annabelle and Andy Wright had been married for years. She was a high-flying lawyer who specialised in financial and criminal law. Avery Zoo had needed her to sort out some of the nastier aspects of the debts Erin Avery had racked up when he'd been running the zoo. I had always assumed that Annabelle and Andy had the perfect marriage - she, the local top lawyer and he, the local historian.

The lead left on the drive suggested otherwise.

"I could talk to her," Auryn offered.

"No, she might not know anything about it. Someone should talk to Andy... but not you."

With Annabelle's fidelity in question and Auryn working so closely with her, his turning up on the historian's doorstep could make matters worse. *Especially if he murdered Timmy,* I thought but dismissed it a moment later. I'd known who the lead belonged to and what it meant before going into the house, and when we'd found poor Timmy it had never even crossed my mind that Andy could be to blame. I asked myself why that was and all I could come up with was that, much like Jon, Andy was just too boring. The mild mannered man I'd met at the barbecue didn't seem capable of flying into a wild rage. If I needed further proof, he'd spent the whole event hanging out with Jon.

"How come Andy's not in the club?" I asked.

"He's not ambitious enough and isn't a legacy of any sort. His family are fairly new money," Jon said, blushing somewhat. He was surely admitting that he was only in the club himself because of some legacy. I didn't know a huge amount about Jon, but ambitious was certainly not a word I'd use to describe him.

"Thanks for doing that," he said, and I smiled at him in return. I hadn't thought a lot of Jon prior to today, but he was starting to grow on me. What I'd thought was a lack of interest in people that only furthered his boringness I now thought might have been shyness. Today he'd proved himself to be loyal and thoughtful.

I realised I'd also mentally discounted Jon as a possible suspect, even though he'd had ample opportunity to pop round Timmy's house prior to picking Auryn and me up. It was the way his face had turned green when he'd seen the body that had done it. No coldblooded killer would have reacted like that, and it really had been a grisly scene. Whoever had done it had been angry.

Now that I thought about it, I felt rather green myself.

Clouds had turned the day overcast when I went back to Avery Zoo with Auryn. It had always been our plan to convene there after the meeting in order to discuss a few forthcoming events our zoos were to collaborate on, but I had a feeling that nothing productive would get done today. It was already close to being the evening and I would have to return to The Lucky Zoo for the evening feeds to cover for the keeper who was unwell. Instead, Auryn and I contented ourselves with getting hot chocolate from the machine in the staffroom and I raided Tiff's supply of whipped cream in order to pimp it up. My locker had been empty for months now, as my place of work was no longer at Avery. I was still there to help oversee breeding programmes and any proposed enclosure changes, but The Lucky Zoo was where most of my attention was focused. Auryn and I even had a friendly little competition going over whose zoo would be the most successful. Avery had a heck of a head-start, and we weren't really competing of course, with most visitors opting for the double zoo pass, but it was still fun to do.

I felt a little pang of nostalgia when I sprayed the squirty cream on the drinks and made a mental note to replenish my best friend's supply. Tiff had been a little distant of late. I'd been ploughing everything into making The Lucky Zoo succeed and she'd been equally busy sorting out the commerce side of things for both of the zoos. I missed her a lot and hoped she was doing okay. Her last boyfriend, Darius, had turned out to be a cheat. Tiff had racked it up as just another case of her making bad choices when it came to men. I'd promised to vet whoever she chose next, but unusually for Tiff, she'd stayed single. I knew it wouldn't be for want of offers, as hardly a day went by without Tiff catching someone's eye, but I did wonder if she was feeling a bit down. And I was a bad friend not knowing for sure.

"Can you believe this?" Auryn said when we were settled in his office with our drinks. "Who would want Timmy dead? He was murdered, right? It looked like it... didn't it?"

I brushed away the implication that I was somehow an expert on these matters. "It looked like someone stabbed him, although I didn't see a weapon. I guess they must have taken it." I bit my lip before continuing, knowing I risked joining the dots. "I wonder when they'll find Scarlett..."

Auryn snorted and then looked embarrassed. "Sorry, I've just known them both longer than you have. When we were younger, I remember Scarlett from the local comprehensive crowd. She was just as wild as Timmy - probably worse. When she knuckled down on her underwear business and Timmy just... well... supported her, I guess everyone thought they'd finally settled down. But then... I knew they were both having flings even before we reconnected. There are people at the zoo who've been involved with one or the other of them at some point in time. Both of them were at it."

"So much for marriage!" I looked anxiously at Auryn.

"You know that will never happen to us. You shouldn't even have to ask it."

"I know, I know... something like this just comes as a surprise. It makes you look at yourself and ask if your life might seem perfect to people looking in but be another story behind closed doors."

"I think our life is pretty perfect," Auryn said with an easy grin.

"I dunno..." I said thoughtfully. Auryn's eyebrows shot

up. "...my life could do with some more whipped cream, but Tiff has run out."

We both took some time out to drink our hot chocolates and Auryn mused that British weather could always be relied upon to throw you a hot chocolate suitable afternoon in the middle of a blazing summer. Sometimes the entirety of a summer would be suitable for hot drinks and blankets.

"You should get some pillows and blankets for your office. I'm going to have some in mine... when I get an office," I amended. The Lucky Zoo had got off to a good start, but my main focus was improving the animal housing part of the zoo. Staff comfort would come next. Fortunately, the group of people I worked with understood and didn't mind hunkering down to work in the old farmhouse until everything was sorted out. Yes, it was surreal having the small human resources team cramped up in the second bedroom with its quaint floral wallpaper, but it was working for now.

"Maybe an office dog, too, or do you think Lucky would mind?" Auryn asked.

"Lucky seems fine with most animals. I bet he could handle a puppy. That reminds me... I think Rameses might be missing. Maybe we should call up to check? With Scarlett missing and Timmy dead, there's no one looking out for him."

"I'll call the police in a bit," Auryn promised. I shot him a look filled with gratitude. After what I'd seen and heard today, one more interference from me would probably get me thrown into a jail cell. It would be a great retirement present for Detective Treesden.

2

CREEPY CRAWLIES

I was about to get in my car to go back to my zoo when I realised where Scarlett was.

Her husband had been due to attend the club meeting and she'd left work early. She was probably with whoever she was currently having an affair with. I turned around and walked back into the office to ask Auryn who that might be.

"Let's try Tristan Saunders first," Auryn said when he announced he'd join me on the quest.

"Do you know what her car looks like?" I asked as we approached Tristan's place of residence.

"Yeah… it's one of those cream Fiat things."

"Tristan Saunders… really?" I said when we pulled up outside of the pub he owned. Tristan had always seemed so happy with his wife, Demi, and their toddler.

"It's just something I heard. You know what gossip is like."

I hoped for Demi Saunders' sake it was nothing more than gossip. I was relieved when we checked the car park behind the pub and didn't see any sign of Scarlett's Fiat.

"Who else?" I asked, swinging the car back onto the road.

Auryn listed a couple of other possibles and we set off. My mouth set in a line when he suggested we check on Jack Lovell. He'd been a part of the team of builders who'd helped Erin Avery smuggle animals out of the zoo to sell on the black market. Although Jack hadn't been involved, I didn't feel overly trusting of him, and I was willing to bet the feeling was mutual.

"Well, that's just great," Auryn said when we pulled into the road where Jack lived and saw the cream Fiat brazenly parked in the driveway.

There was a silent argument as I pointed at Auryn and he pointed at me and we gestured at one another before Auryn got out of the car. Auryn had been responsible for the termination of future contracts with the company that Jack worked for, but I was the one who'd actually put his buddies in prison. I reckoned that meant I would be the least popular choice of person to interrupt a pleasant day spent with a fling.

I watched Auryn as he went up and rang the bell. A moment later, a man in a dressing gown answered it. When he saw Auryn, things immediately took a bad turn. It was all too obvious they were arguing. I got out of the car, figuring I couldn't make things too much worse.

"Just tell Scarlett to get out here now," Auryn was saying.

The man shot a dark look my way. "What makes you think she's here?"

"Her car's right in your driveway. If you want to keep something a secret, learn a little subtlety."

Jack shrugged. "It doesn't matter. It won't be quiet for long. I might well be one of the family soon." A dreamy smile came onto his face.

"If you believe that, you're even dumber than you look," Auryn said, scoffing at the idea.

"Who are you to say?" the other man protested.

"Put it this way… yours wasn't the first house we visited when we came looking for Scarlett."

His face dropped. For a brief moment, I thought he might take a swing at Auryn, but he turned and yelled back into the house for Scarlett to come to the door. She appeared a moment later dressed in suit trousers and a blouse with an exceedingly annoyed expression on her face.

"What are you doing here?" she asked, but our faces surely gave away that it was serious. She stepped outside without another word of protest.

"Well, what is it?" she asked when Jack had slammed the door behind her.

I looked across at Auryn, both of us realising that we had inadvertently made it so that we had to deliver the bad news.

"It's Timmy… I'm afraid he's dead," I said, as carefully as I could.

The impressive blonde woman in front of me froze. Her face could have been carved out of marble - a beautiful piece of marble that showed the benefits of a fortune spent on surgical procedures, but marble nonetheless.

"Dead?" she repeated, her emotions giving nothing away.

"Yes, and the police are looking for you." I couldn't spell it out much more obviously than that.

Scarlett's expression immediately clouded. "Do you think I should call a lawyer?"

I thought about it. "Maybe… but not Annabelle Wright," I hastily added, remembering the lead on the drive.

Scarlett shot me a quizzical look but didn't ask. "Okay, I'll text one of my company's lawyers. Then I'll grab a couple of things and go to the police."

"You can't go home," Auryn said. "It's a crime scene. That's where we found him."

"What was he doing? Why was he at home?" Her concern

had turned to suspicion, I noted. As I'd suspected, Scarlett was very aware that her husband had been cheating on her.

"We're not sure. It looked like someone attacked him." I bit my tongue, knowing I shouldn't say too much more.

"Poor, poor Timmy. He was always in the wrong place at the wrong time." Scarlett smiled a little fondly for a moment. "How did the attacker get in?"

"We're not sure," Auryn said.

To our surprise... a car pulled across the driveway behind my Fiesta. For a brief moment, my belly flip-flopped around as I feared the police had located Scarlett, too, and we were going to be dragged over hot coals for tipping-off a potential suspect.

A well-dressed woman got out of the car and marched over to us. "You're lucky I was just on my way to see you about the contract. Now, what's all this about a murder?" She inspected Auryn and me from behind her stunningly on-trend glasses and hair that surely saw a hairdresser once a week, rather than the once every couple of months mine got.

"This is my lawyer, Georgina Farley," Scarlett supplied.

When the 'pleased to meet yous' were over, the woman renewed her severe gaze upon us. I realised she was waiting for an answer to her first question.

"Timmy Marsden has died. We believe he was probably murdered. The police are still looking for her." I inclined my head in Scarlett's direction.

Georgina Farley's face gave nothing away when she nodded succinctly to show that she understood the situation. "I'm going to stop you right there. Scarlett, wait in the car. We'll discuss what you know in private, so that we're not going to be tripped up in questioning. I don't want Scarlett to have any more knowledge than she should have." She waited for the car door to slam. "What do you know?"

"Just what we told you," Auryn jumped in. "He's dead, and it looks like someone maybe broke in and attacked him."

"How do you figure that?" Georgina asked.

"The front door was unlocked," Auryn explained.

"The patio door was, too, although - that's less unusual. Timmy was about to go out, and he might have wanted to let the dog out one last time before leaving. His body was in front of the patio door," I told her.

"How do you think the intruder got in?" the lawyer quizzed.

I thought about it. "The patio door. Timmy was on his back with his feet facing the door and the damage was done to the front of his chest. I think someone probably came through there, stabbed him, and he fell backwards."

"Who would have access to that door?" The lawyer shot me a look that said 'other than my client, obviously...'.

"Well, there are hedges on the sides of the house, but there's also a garden gate that leads down the side of the house. It was open when we were there for the barbecue."

"There's the footpath, too. A fence goes along the bottom of the garden, but it's not that high. It's just supposed to keep Rameses in. There's also a gate in the fence, to access the public footpath for dog walks and stuff, I guess," Auryn said. "I asked Timmy about it when I saw people down there when I was round one time."

"So, ample opportunity for someone - anyone - to access those doors. Thank you," Georgina said making sure to look us both in the eye when she said it. She was a pro all right.

We turned back towards the cars where Scarlett was waiting. The very recently widowed woman opened the door.

"We need to head over to the police station. Take your car, Scarlett. I'm sure I don't have to tell you why you don't want to be seen picking it up from here later on," the lawyer said.

"I hope none of this affects Jack. He's just starting his own business. I'd hate for his reputation to suffer," Scarlett fretted. I felt like bopping her over the head. Her husband had probably been murdered and she was more worried about how it might damage her lover's reputation? If I were her, I'd be more concerned by the very real possibility that the police were going to lock me up for murder.

"He will need to be involved. You need an alibi," Georgina said. She was still managing to keep everything blank, but I'd been watching her over the past couple of minutes and I thought I could tell she found Scarlett's attitude on this matter trying.

Georgina turned to us before getting in her car. "Thank you again for your help. I'll let you know if I have any further questions..." She left it hanging, and I realised she was waiting for contact details.

"Just contact Avery Zoo or The Lucky Zoo and ask for Auryn or Madi, respectively. We're not hard to find," my fiancé helpfully said.

"Quite," Georgina said, looking at me with interest. I had a shrewd idea she'd already known who I was. My own renown still surprised me.

When the lawyer had raced off, I backed out to let Scarlett follow her.

"Did we do a good thing or a really bad thing?" Auryn said, voicing my own thoughts aloud.

I shook my head. "I have no idea."

The next morning, I woke up to a boatload of responsibility that I'd completely forgotten about. It was Monday and as soon as I opened my eyes I remembered I was holding interviews today… and I hadn't done a thing to prepare. I'd planned to spend an hour or so the previous evening, coming up with pertinent questions to ask my prospective employees, but after seeing Timmy Marsden's final resting place on the kitchen floor, Auryn and I had sought comfort in a bottle of wine. Or had it been two? My dry mouth hinted at the truth.

I pushed myself upright and saw the time on the quaint alarm clock Auryn kept by the bed. To top things off, I'd overslept.

"Auryn I've got interviews today. I forgot to prepare," I said, nudging my fiancé awake.

He opened one grey eye. "Just wing it. It will be fine."

"Really?"

"I dunno. As part of the zoo's 'everyone takes part' ethos, the managers do the interviewing and I pop in during the final round in order to make everyone feel special and to win myself 'future boss' brownie points."

I looked at him. "That sounds pretty cynical."

"I'm just a coldhearted businessman at heart." He waited to see if I was buying it. I wasn't. "I get nosy," he confessed. "The only interviews I'd personally conduct would be for management positions. Since taking over, there's only been one of those interviews needed."

We both paused for a moment of silence, remembering the old head of reception, Jenna, who'd died before Christmas.

"What did you ask in that interview? I need some help here!"

"I asked general stuff. I don't even remember. It was just like having a conversation." The infuriating thing was, I believed him. Auryn was a natural people-person.

I was not.

"What jobs are you even interviewing for?" Auryn asked, propping himself up with an elbow and looking for all the world like he might have just jumped off the cover of a cheesy romance novel. I would certainly buy it.

I reluctantly dragged my focus back to the looming disaster. "I need a reptile and amphibians keeper... at least Vanessa is sitting in with me for that one," I said, referring to Avery Zoo's expert in all things that had extra legs, no legs, or scales. "The other position is for an in-house marketing-cum-PR expert."

"Do you really need one?" Auryn asked. I'd been outsourcing the zoo's marketing since opening. Auryn often used external companies to help promote certain events, but he also had a small team at the zoo. They weren't necessarily experts, as most of them were technically reception and HR workers, but they got things done. My zoo didn't even have that much.

"I thought it would be good to try and hand it over to someone else. Although, I'm not convinced I'll find someone who can do it all. Especially considering the salary I'm offering..." I hesitated. "Am I being stingy?"

"No," Auryn said, pushing himself fully upright. "When you employ someone, you let them know the job has good prospects. If you employ someone and they prove their worth, then there's the potential for pay rises and promotions. You can't give it all away to someone who hasn't shown you their worth yet."

"Thanks, you're right." I was definitely suffering from a spot of nerves.

"You'll do fine," Auryn promised me.

I tried to look half as confident as he sounded.

I'd scheduled the reptiles, amphibians, and all things crawly interviews for the morning. With a keeper as experienced as Vanessa by my side, I was confident we'd make a good choice. So far, we'd seen two potential keepers. I'd thought that both interviewees were friendly and enthusiastic and had marked them as possibles. However, I'd been able to tell that Vanessa hadn't been impressed. The Avery Zoo zookeeper was odd to say the least, but I trusted her judgement completely. Avery Zoo's collection of reptiles, amphibians, and insects may be small, but I knew it was of a very high standard.

I shuffled my papers while Vanessa went out to show the next person in.

A young woman with a neat bob and a strangely blank face sat down in front of us. If I'd had to describe her, I would have likened her to a lizard. Everything about her was still and expressionless, but her eyes were bright and made me more than a little uneasy.

"I'm Gabby Snow," the woman introduced herself, thrusting out a hand towards me before I'd gathered myself up to do the same. I reached and then recoiled when I saw something move on her sleeve.

She looked down. "Oh! There you are, Entwhistle! I thought I'd lost you." She picked off the creepy critter.

"What a wonderful example of an Indian stick insect!" Vanessa said, jumping to her feet and holding her hands out to receive the twiggy-looking thing.

I watched and attempted to share her admiration. Then I gave up. There were limits to my desire to care for animals. That was why it was so essential that I found a keeper who did want to specialise in this area.

I watched as the interview deviated wildly from any planned questions and instead revolved around the weird and wonderful pets the two women had. I did my best to make sure I asked about Gabby's prior experience and what she thought of the zoo, but I already knew we'd found the right woman for the job. She wasn't particularly people friendly, and she certainly gave me the willies, but then... so did Vanessa.

"Hire her," Vanessa said as soon as Gabby Snow had left the room. Then, she stood up and walked out, leaving me to deal with the other few applicants alone. See what I mean about not people-friendly? Apparently things weren't going to get any better than a woman who walked in carrying a stick insect and then chattered at great length about the chameleons she bred for fun and frolics.

Once the morning zookeeper interviews were over and I'd called Gabby Snow back almost immediately to offer her the job (she'd accepted) it was time to find my marketing miracle worker. My suspicions that the salary offered and vague job description hadn't attracted the highest calibre of applicants were confirmed when I looked out at the strange mix of interviewees. A few were probably teenagers, fresh out of school and hoping to try their luck. Then there were the slightly more senior, but equally desperate, university students. Finally, there were a handful of what I suspected were probably mums who'd been attracted by the potential of flexible hours. I pushed my disappointment deep down and reminded myself that appearances could be deceptive. If one of my applicants was an eighteen year old marketing and public relations genius with a billion social media followers and brilliant ideas, I was certainly going to give them a chance.

Unfortunately, the first few interviews mirrored my initial perceptions and not my hopes. The teenagers just wanted to work on Facebook all day and couldn't tell me anything about how effective the platform was for actually generating event sign ups, or attracting people to the zoo. We had a Facebook page and one of the admin staff at Avery who dealt with the other zoo's stuff posted to our page daily, too, and it had a good amount of likes and engagement. The Lucky Zoo didn't need a huge amount of work there, it needed fresh ideas and someone with a passion to see them through (I'd abandoned any hope of employing someone with a huge level of experience as soon as I'd seen the lineup).

Worse than the teenagers were the newly graduated bunch. They seemed to believe that spouting technical jargon and figures taken from irrelevant giant corporations were going to baffle me into giving them the job.

The mums were the group I was most hopeful about. A couple of them had some good prior experience, and I was sure that having to cope with kids meant their creativity and problem solving skills were going to be off the charts. The only thing that was making me hesitate was knowing they would never be able to put in extra time when the zoo needed it, and also, I didn't get the sense from any of them that they particularly wanted a career with the potential for advancements. They wanted something that plodded along.

By the middle of the afternoon, I was losing the will to live. My thoughts kept drifting back to the crime scene I'd witnessed yesterday, even though I'd done a fairly effective job of blocking it out so far. I was just wondering if Scarlett's lawyer had managed to get her back out of the police station, or if she was sitting in a cell, when someone knocked on the door.

I looked up and discovered a man in his thirties, dressed in jeans and a t-shirt, standing there. He was too old to be someone fresh out of school and even though I knew mature students existed, he didn't give off any whiff of shiny new graduate either - the lack of a try-hard suit was evidence enough of that. He seemed to exude confidence from his broad frame.

I couldn't place him at all.

"Are you here for the interview?" I asked, not recognising this man as any of the potentials I'd reached out to for an interview.

"What interview would that be?" he asked, throwing me for the second time.

"It's for someone to do the zoo's marketing and PR. Sort of like asking for a superhero," I confessed, having realised I had to be asking too much.

"I could probably do that," the casually-dressed man said, gracefully seating himself opposite the desk I'd set up.

"But that wasn't why you came here?" I was getting more confused by the second.

"I came here because I heard about the new zoo and I'm in the market for a job. I thought I could get in on the ground floor, so to speak, if I came in and asked if you had any positions going and handed in my CV." He took a sheaf of paper out of the briefcase he'd been carrying.

I glanced at the summary. "You sound very well-qualified." I looked up at his serious eyes that seemed to be completely colourless, taking on the shades of the environment around him. "I should probably give you the job description to see if it's something you'd be willing to consider..." I hoped I wasn't blushing too obviously. I knew that the salary listed wasn't going to be anywhere close to what this man must have come to expect. I didn't think anyone in the zoo would ever be on that kind of money, myself included, if you cancelled out the comic income. "It is of course open to negotiation," I added when I handed over the description.

He scanned the page. "Looks good. I want to work from home on some days and come in on others. I've just left a city job and I'm looking to have some more 'me' time."

"No kids?" I asked, wanting to find out if he was just

covering for the fact that he was a stay-at-home dad. I had no problem with that, but I did like people to be upfront with me.

He shook his head and there was something about him that made me feel it was a ridiculous question to have asked. On the surface, this man seemed normal. He was a little better looking than average and possessed a lovely head of steel-grey hair. Broad shoulders and a slightly stocky stature that hinted of exercise meant he wouldn't have looked out of place in the forces.

Yes, there was definitely something that said without a doubt he wasn't going to settle down and play house. But did that same something make it anymore likely he wanted a job at a rural zoo and 'me' time?

"I'm Pierce Goodman, by the way," he said, extending a hand. I shook it, realising I'd let the conversation lapse.

"Madigan Amos, but please, call me Madi."

"Well, Madi, I would love to be considered. If you could agree to the working from home on some days and a salary that's…" he looked at the page "…ten grand more than that, I'd be on board." He fixed me with a look. "Trust me. I am worth the money."

I did my best to smile back at him. Somehow, I didn't doubt that he was telling the truth, but there was still something about this man I wasn't sure about. It was probably the way he'd made talking about running marketing campaigns and PR exercises sound just as serious as employing an assassin to take out a business rival. In fact, Pierce looked like the kind of guy you might ask to do exactly that.

"Have you got any ideas of what you might do for the zoo, if you're chosen?" I was determined to get this strange interview back on track.

Pierce continued to look at me with his strange unerring eye contact, like I was the one being interviewed rather than the other way around. "My ideas would include getting people to come to the zoo and promoting any events you want promoted so that they sell out."

I opened my mouth to ask how exactly he'd do it and then shut it again. Who else did I have on my possibles list when every interview prior to this one had been a disaster? Sure, this man wanted an extra 10K a year, but I hadn't been sure what a fair salary was anyway, and more to the point... I was curious.

"What would you say to a one month trial period?" There, I wasn't going to get myself in too deep.

"Sounds great. I'll see you tomorrow. You can take me through what's going on in the zoo and anything technical. I'll take it from there."

I really didn't know whether this man was my saviour or my downfall. Had I really just offered him a job, or had he just assumed it? "I'll see you tomorrow at nine," I said, stamping my authority one last time. The amusement that flashed across his eyes said he knew it.

"Fine. Looking forward to working with you." We shook hands again and then he left without waiting for me to ask if he had any questions or... what else was I supposed to have done? After the earlier interviews, I'd felt I'd been getting the hang of this stuff, but then this man had walked in, apparently not even for the interview, and had walked out with the job.

"He's probably just what the zoo needs," I said aloud.

But that's what bothered me most of all about Pierce Goodman. He was too right for the job.

I sighed and sat back in my chair in the office I'd put together for myself in the empty, but impressive, barn conversion. The Abraham family, who were responsible for most of the zoo's design and concept, had converted the barn and then lived there up until their mysterious disappearance.

That mystery had since been solved and the truth found to be a grisly one, but I'd thought it was about time that the building was used again. That was why I'd taken the decision to move the bedroom furniture out of what had been the spare room and set up an office for the interviews today. When things were more organised, I promised myself that the conversion would be used for further offices and perhaps a conservation and education programme, too. I wanted The Lucky Zoo to be just as educational as Avery was.

"Hold your horses," I muttered to myself. It was great to have big plans, but I knew full well I was getting ahead of myself. The Lucky Zoo had a long way to go and businesses weren't built in a day. First, we had to impress with our animal care and interest. Then we could turn our attention to nuances like education - the icing on the cake.

I bit my lip when my mind drifted back to the perfect job applicant. I was almost certain I was just being incredibly paranoid... but what if? Could he be more than he appeared? I'd already mentally compared his physique to that of someone who'd worked in the forces. Then there was the fact that he was wildly suitable - incredibly so - when everyone else had been uninspiring. What were the chances of someone who appeared as slick and formidable at their job as he did being interested in such a lowly position here? I knew there was potential for advancement, but it was clear Pierce Goodman wasn't on the first job of his career. And I also didn't think he just wanted to take some time out from the rat race.

I did some more lip biting before I dialled Katya's number. MI5 had asked her to keep watch on me when I'd gone on holiday to Mallorca with Auryn. Now that I was back, did I really believe that they were willing to just let me go about my life like a normal person, as if nothing had ever happened? The way Katya had talked about it, she'd implied they still believed I had contact with my old fake publishing company, who'd turned out to be a gang of money launderers. On the one hand, I was amused that British Intelligence thought I had enough free time to be dabbling in a life of crime, but on the other, it was exceedingly annoying that they felt the need to monitor me. There were a couple of people I'd met in their organisation that I'd definitely rubbed up the wrong way. Perhaps even now they weren't willing to let it go.

Or perhaps I'd finally snapped and gone bat-poo crazy.

The call went to voicemail. I didn't leave a message. Katya and I were not supposed to be friends. After everything that had happened and the way I'd been deceived, I was sure any sane person would never trust someone they knew to be working for the intelligence service again, but I did trust Katya. That was why I wanted to call her to ask if she could clue me in on whether or not Pierce Goodman was anything to do with them.

After thinking about it some more, I was actually glad that Katya hadn't answered. I really did believe she was my friend, but what kind of friend would I be if I only ever called her to ask her to fill me in on official business? She wasn't my informant!

I sat back in my chair with Pierce's CV. If there was anything fishy about my newest employee, I would have to find out what it was for myself. And so, with no little trepidation, I dialled the first number on Pierce's list of references.

3

SPARKS FLY

"Hey, have you heard anything more about Timmy?" I greeted Auryn when he came down to breakfast the next morning. Yesterday had turned into a busy one for both of us, and I'd stayed up late trying to catch up on my comic work, so there hadn't exactly been any quality time between us.

"Not that I've heard. I suppose they're probably piecing what they have together. Or perhaps they already think they know who did it." Auryn shot me a knowing look. "Scarlett might have just arrived at her lover's house, for all we know. He certainly struck me as stupid enough to lie for her if she asked him."

"They'll need more evidence if that is the case," I observed.

Auryn shrugged. "I guess we'll all have to wait and see. I almost hope it is Scarlett and she's locked up. Otherwise, there's a killer walking free who none of us knows about."

I poured myself a bowl of cornflakes (no chocolate raisins this morning) and added milk, trying not to think about that chilling concept. "I managed to find two new

50

employees," I said, changing the subject onto more cheerful ground. "The new zookeeper got on really well with Vanessa, so she's probably a great choice..." I waited for Auryn to get it.

"You mean she's really weird and a bit creepy?"

"Bingo. I also found someone for the other job, the one I was worrying about."

"What are they like?"

"That's a good question..." I explained about Pierce's surprising entrance and how he'd basically sold me on the job. "I mean, if he can convince me to give him the job that quickly, I think he'll probably be as good as his word on the other stuff. I called a couple of his references and they only spoke of him in glowing terms." I kept my expression blank, but Auryn knew me too well.

"Were you not sure about him?"

"He just seemed... too perfect for the job, you know? I have this feeling like he could be working for some giant successful business who can afford to keep him in lobster and caviar for eternity. Why on earth would he want to work at a zoo? And a zoo that's just starting out! It hardly screams fantastic pay and a reliable career."

"Perhaps he wanted something different," Auryn said, playing devil's advocate.

"Well... maybe. I just couldn't help but wonder..."

The front doorbell rang. I was closest, so I got up. Lucky ran ahead, apparently a lot more eager to see who was calling at this rather early hour than I was.

"Is Auryn here?"

It took me a couple of moments to realise who the woman standing on the doorstep was. She was dressed in a classy, but efficient, ensemble. Her blouse, although silky, was not flashy, and even her hair, pulled back into a bun at the nape of her neck, hinted that she was more focused on hitting goals than creative makeup and hair. I could definitely respect that.

"You're Annabelle Wright, aren't you?" I hadn't actually met the lawyer Auryn had sought advice from for some of Avery Zoo's debts.

"I am," she confirmed, giving me a look that let me know she knew full well who I was and needed no introduction. "Auryn?" she prompted when I carried on looking at her and doing nothing.

"Come in, Annabelle. What can I do for you?" Auryn asked, having arrived behind me. Courteous as ever, he then offered her some coffee.

"I'm not staying long. I just came to ask... is it true? Is Timmy dead? I heard it from a friend of a friend, but no one's saying anything for sure. I drove by the house and saw there was police tape, but he's really dead?"

"He is," Auryn confirmed with an appropriate level of solemness. I was mostly focusing on not raising my eyebrows at her line of enquiry, suspecting what I did about Annabelle's relationship with Timmy Marsden.

"That's terrible! Why on earth is it being kept quiet? A popular man like Timmy will have a huge funeral. He had so many friends..."

"The police are still investigating his death. They must have their own reasons for keeping it quiet for now," I told her.

"You think he was murdered?" Annabelle wasn't a lawyer for nothing.

Auryn and I looked at one another and then nodded. No one had actually asked us to stay silent about what we'd seen, although I knew neither of us was going to spread it around.

All of a sudden, Annabelle's face crumpled. A tear slipped down her cheek. "I just can't believe it. He was going to leave his ridiculous wife for me, you know. Both of us are caught in sham marriages. He was divorced in all but name, let me assure you..."

I blinked at her sudden change of tone from heartbroken to venomous.

"That's so sad," I said, hoping Auryn wasn't going to fall over in surprise at my sudden uncharacteristic attack of empathy. "When did you last see Timmy?"

"Oh, it was on Saturday night. Scarlett was out partying with the work people because of some deal that was going to go through - at least, that's the line she'd spun Timmy. Bless his heart. I'm still not sure if he actually believed her or not. I suppose now we'll never know..." The lawyer sighed.

I privately thought that Timmy, albeit occasionally buffoonish, had been pretty smart. He'd known that Scarlett was messing around, just as she knew he was. If he'd been trying to convince Annabelle otherwise, he was going for the sympathy vote.

"What about the next morning - Sunday? Did you stay round?" I asked.

The lawyer's gaze immediately sharpened. As I'd mentioned before, she was no dummy. "I was at Avery Zoo running a workshop for the HR department on how to talk yourself out of getting sued. I'm expanding my business," she informed me with a hint of danger in her voice. The lawyer's lips thinned. "In my experience, which is plentiful, it's always the spouse. How was he killed?"

"We think stabbed," I said, figuring it probably didn't matter. Surely the police would be making that information public soon, and I also didn't see how the method of murder would give away the killer.

Annabelle sighed. "We finally find each other and then something like this happens."

I did my best to keep from rolling my eyes. Annabelle may be good at law, but she seemed to be terrible at noticing what was going on right under her nose. Timmy did not strike me as a one-woman man. In turn, Scarlett had struck me as a blonde whirlwind of a woman - the kind who could entrance men and keep them on tenterhooks no matter where her loyalties really lay. Annabelle surely hadn't stood a real chance against that.

"I don't mean to overstep our professional boundaries," Auryn said, tactful as ever, "but you're married! You have a family!"

Annabelle had the good grace to look a little embarrassed. "It's complicated," she said, airily. Which I privately thought was lawyer speak for none of your business. I wondered if she knew that her husband was well aware of her affair. I wondered if her own life could be in danger because of that...

"I think you should go," Auryn told his lawyer in a polite but firm way.

Annabelle stared at him in surprise and then seemed to recover herself, maybe realising all of what she'd said. "Yes, of course. I just wanted to be sure. I didn't want to believe it."

Auryn shut the door behind her and then turned to me with disbelief written across his face.

"Someone needs to talk to her husband. We can't keep quiet about it forever," I told him.

He nodded thoughtfully. "You should do it."

"What? Why me?"

"The guy's a historian who writes books. You're a famous writer. Kind of," he added.

"How dare you! Comic book writing is every bit as much writing as writing is." I felt myself stumbling over my words and reflected that perhaps it was fortunate after all that comic books only had small spaces for very succinct comments.

Auryn grinned having baited me into giving him the very answer he'd desired.

"Fine. But it's your fault if I get murdered," I told him.

The next day I pulled up outside Avery Zoo with my two new employees in my car. I'd given them the grand tour of The Lucky Zoo, which had taken most of the morning. Now it was time to introduce them to our sister zoo. While they probably wouldn't be spending much time here, I thought it was important that they both saw the standards to which we were all aspiring. Avery had experience and a polished finish. My zoo needed to play some serious catchup.

I took them round all of the animal areas, hoping to give Gabby a feel for Vanessa's brilliant work and to give Pierce an idea of how well-presented a zoo could be. The Lucky Zoo was impressive to look at, due to its groundbreaking eco design, but the way Avery used its best features in marketing and special events would, I hoped, become obvious to him.

Halfway round, Gabby became engrossed in the insect house and I made the executive decision to leave her behind with instructions to meet back at the car later. She wouldn't benefit from this next part anyway.

"I thought it might be useful if you were to meet the head of commerce at Avery Zoo. I know that's hardly the same as marketing and PR and that stuff," I bumbled, remembering there was a good reason why I was hiring someone to do this for me, "but she's in charge of a lot of revenue generation, and I thought you might be able to bounce some of your ideas off her."

"Sure," Pierce said, amiably enough. I didn't miss the slight smile on his lips. He knew I was pushing him to reveal something - anything - about what he was going to do in his new role. Half of me wanted to just throw my hands up and say 'get on with it' and wait to see what happened. So long as it wasn't illegal and it worked, I'd be happy with that. The other half of me wanted to kick Pierce, who was surely being deliberately secretive. It was maddening.

But if anyone could persuade him to confide, I was certain that Tiff was the right choice.

My best friend walked out of the shop, right on cue. "Hi Madi! Hello," she said, turning her bright smile on Pierce.

It was like watching a car crash in slow motion. First, there was the shock then the dawning realisation that there was no way you were getting out of this unscathed. I'd seen it on men's faces many times before when Tiff walked into their lives. Now I was seeing it happen to Pierce.

"I'm Pierce," he said, holding out a hand and shaking Tiff's for a lot longer than he had mine when we'd first met. Some men went to pieces when they were faced with my beautiful friend, but something told me that Pierce was merely taking things up a gear.

"It's nice to meet you." Tiff kept smiling and, a little more unusually, I could tell she was taken aback by Pierce the same way he was with her. Well, well! Perhaps there had been something to gain by their introduction after all. My new PR and marketing guru could be good for both the zoo and my best friend, who was still mourning the loss of her cheating ex.

"How about I leave you talking about your success with the commerce at Avery. I'll go get a drink and come back later," I said, coming to the conclusion that my presence wasn't necessary or desired.

When Tiff shot me a laser look, I realised I'd probably been a bit too obvious.

"Don't forget, you and Auryn owe me some squirty

cream. And throw in some marshmallows for the trauma caused, too!" was all she said.

"How about a lifetime's supply of fancy hot drinks once the restaurant opens?" I offered.

"You don't know what you've just got yourself into. Deal!" Tiff announced with a grin so broad, I did wonder if she would prove to be correct. Her smile lessened a little when she remembered Pierce's presence and clearly wanted to appear more demure and less like a woman with a whipped cream addiction. I decided to let my partner in hot chocolate drinking off, just this once. I nodded goodbye and left them to it.

All of the talk about the restaurant opening had reminded me I needed to go check on its progress. Auryn had been keeping me up to date on my newest investment, but I wanted to see the progress for myself. After all - I had a bet to win!

Auryn believed that, in spite of the larger initial investment, The Lucky Zoo would have made back the purchase cost before the restaurant I was rebuilding would have recouped the money I'd fronted. I knew Auryn didn't believe the restaurant would actually ever make back what it was costing to rebuild it, but I had big plans for it.

Before a bomb had quite literally gone off inside of the building, the restaurant itself had never been very successful. It had been an afterthought. Customers were already in the zoo, why not fleece them for lunch, too? As this had been the guiding inspiration, predictably, it hadn't gone very well. The only time people had ever graced the restaurant in large numbers had been on Valentine's Day, when they'd left it too late to book anywhere else.

I was determined that this time it would be different.

As well as making our fun little wager, the restaurant was also the only idea Auryn and I had been able to come up with for our wedding venue. I wasn't the kind of girl who wanted a huge white wedding, but the restaurant-cum-wedding-venue sure as heck wasn't going to be plastic foliage glued to walls and creepy stuffed animals that screeched at you when you walked past. It was going to be classy. Fortunately, with the first volume of my comic *Monday's Menagerie* still flying off the shelves, I could definitely afford to make it so.

I was watching the builders adding render to the outside walls when I saw Claudia, the zoo's financial advisor, walking towards me. The relationship between us was a little tenuous, so I did my best to look happy to see her.

"I heard that you were the one who found Timmy Marsden. Tough break," she began. Already my heart had sunk a mile. Did everyone know the deceased?!

"Technically, it was Auryn who found him," I said for want of something better to say.

"It was bound to happen sooner or later."

I blinked and stared at Claudia. Did she know something about his murder?

"I just mean he got around a lot, you know? Everyone does it, of course, but he was particularly brazen," she continued.

"I'm sorry... everyone does it?" Was she about to give any specific examples?

"Well, there's just no loyalty these days, is there? It's the new norm," Claudia stated matter-of-factly.

I was still thinking of how to answer that without finding myself falling out with Claudia all over again when Auryn arrived. I wasn't sure if that was good timing or very very bad.

"It's looking great, isn't it?" he said, nodding to the restaurant-in-progress. The exterior needs a little prettying up, but the inside is basically ready. Again, a few interior design features wouldn't go amiss, but I reckon you could start serving food and drinks almost immediately. The kitchen's in and wired up." He leant in closer so I would be the only one to hear the next part. "It's amazing how quickly money achieves things. Don't forget our bet!"

I grinned at him. I hadn't. The sooner the restaurant started functioning as a restaurant, the sooner it would be making back my money.

Auryn stepped back and cleared his throat. There was something about his face that made Claudia make her excuses and leave us to it. When she was gone, Auryn's expression turned serious. "Timmy Marsden's brother and wife are coming into town later today. They need somewhere to stay - somewhere with friends, as they're understandably distressed. Jon would have offered, but his house is full of kids and he can't really accommodate a couple of extra guests. Apparently, everyone else who was friends with Timmy is currently hiding under a rock." He looked peeved. "Some friends they're turning out to be."

"I suppose they want to wait to see who gets collared for the crime. They probably don't want to get involved." I was thinking about Scarlett when I said it. Her and Timmy's friends could be one and the same. They were probably all considering that she might soon end up in prison. I frowned. "Have you heard anything more about Timmy?"

Auryn shook his head. "The brother and wife coming is the latest I've heard. I'm sure we'll find out more, once they've been down to the station." He waggled his eyebrows. "See? Looking after them will have its benefits."

"Well, we can't deny the house is big enough. We could put them on the top floor and never even know they were with us," I joked. Auryn's family's house was far too large for a couple. There were rooms we never went into that were just left to decay. We both knew it was an unsuitable place to be living, but I also understood that for Auryn, it would be tricky to let go of one of the last ties to his family that he possessed, along with the zoo.

With his father in prison and his granddad recently deceased, Auryn was essentially on his own. His mother had divorced his father long before he'd been in trouble with the law, but I now understood that it hadn't been an amiable break up. Erin had insisted that Auryn would take over the zoo and had somehow managed to win custody. His ex-wife now had her own family and was living somewhere far, far away. Auryn rarely spoke of her, and from the little that he'd said, I gathered that far from being proud of him for rescuing the struggling zoo, she resented that he'd stepped into the shoes his father had been polishing for him all along. She must have the rest of Auryn's relatives on side, too, because I hadn't seen hide nor hair of cousins, aunts, or uncles. Auryn might have received his inheritance early, but he had been left on his own to enjoy it.

"What about mother?" I asked, suddenly realising that if his brother was coming, shouldn't she be coming, too?

"She died when his dad did a few years ago, right before Timmy was due to head off to university after his gap year. There was this huge hunting accident that made the news and everything. Horses had to be put down and the two fatalities were Timmy's parents." He shook his head. "At least they died doing what they loved."

"Murdering foxes? Great," I said, unimpressed.

Auryn shot me a sideways look. "You might want to sit on thoughts like that one when these two arrive, and if you're around anyone who knew Timmy. It might be illegal, but fox hunting is still a huge sport in certain circles."

"You've never... have you?" I was shocked that I even

needed to have this conversation with my fiancé. I'd just assumed he was a reasonable human being.

"No, of course not. I'm not a fan of bloodsports. I do miss horse riding, though," he admitted.

"I never knew you liked riding!"

Auryn gave me a wry smile. "It was practically part of the curriculum at the school I went to with all of the other boys. There used to be stables in the garden at the house. My mother took the horses with her when she left, and my father had the stables demolished soon after. I suppose it was his way of accepting she was never coming back." He snapped out of his thoughtful reverie the way I noticed he always seemed to when talking about his parents. "Anyway, that's fine, isn't it? Having these people stay with us?"

I nodded. It was Auryn's house, and it would be nice to do a good turn for the recently bereaved. "Perhaps they'll know who might have wanted to kill Timmy," I said, voicing my thoughts aloud.

"Do not say anything like that to them!"

"I promise I'll be on my best behaviour. After all, murder is a serious crime." I narrowed my eyes thoughtfully. "And someone has to answer for that crime."

Auryn had uncertainty written across his face. "You just focus on your restaurant menu. We have a bet!"

Unfortunately for my wager, I had more pressing matters to attend to once I'd retrieved Pierce from Tiff's charming company and dragged Gabby away from the hissing cockroaches. After setting them up to work and reminding them that they could call me at any time with questions, I went back to the house to prepare the guest bedroom and dive into the other aspect of my life - my comic.

I hadn't got off to the best start with my current publishers. Without consulting me, they'd assigned me a publicist, who had crossed enough personal privacy lines for the Mallorca police to find there was a legitimate reason to arrest him for stalking. I'd offered to drop the case if the publicist was dropped from the publishing house's payroll. They had grudgingly agreed and had later apologised. Whilst I had been keeping a close eye on things ever since, there hadn't been any further deal-breaking problems. I'd done my fair share of press ops, interviews, and school visits, and in return, my publishers had continued to promote my comic book and say what a wonderful storyteller and artist I was. `

All that had been great until they'd asked if the next book was ready yet.

Part of my publishing deal was that I was permitted to continue writing and posting my comic strips on my webcomic site, where people could read them for free. To avoid crossover, I'd agreed to write separate storylines from the same comic, which made up the publishable work that people would buy in paperback and hardback. What I'd essentially done was create double the amount of work for myself.

I didn't mind writing and drawing the comic. *Monday's Menagerie* had, after all, started out as a hobby. It wasn't the most painful thing to turn into work. But I was aware that juggling a comic that had become something of a global phenomenon, and a new zoo that still needed a lot of hand-holding to get it through the early stages, was a heck of a big ask. Most people would have struggled to keep just one of those occupations going, but here I was, thinking I could handle both.

I shook my head and opened my comic sketchbook. I'd had a long bargaining session with my publisher about just when the next book would be ready. At first, I'd kicked against a fresh one being in the shops by Christmas, but after a few concessions on the part of my publisher - including rushed printing so I had a longer deadline - I'd agreed. It was still going to be tight, but I'd found more time than I'd expected in-between long hours worked at the zoo, and the comic strips were coming on well.

I was really hopeful that readers of my traditionally published comic were going to enjoy the deviation into marine animals that the storyline had taken - courtesy of my time spent at The Big Blue Marine Park. After what had happened, I'd been determined to take something good away from the experience. I smiled as I flicked through the pages and stopped at one where cartoon Lucky was tentatively dipping his paw into a shark tank, whilst a toothy shark looked up with menace. Fortunately, I knew my comic book cat would make a great escape and a witty joke before the panels ended.

Real life Lucky jumped up onto my lap and bumped my chin with his head. I stroked him with a free hand and reflected that there wasn't long to go before he was a whole year old. His kitten days were over and his feline thirst for blood was awakening big time. When he'd first been let out, he'd mostly brought back leaves, and then a few mice. Now we were out further in the country, he'd made it his mission to wreak terrible furry vengeance on the local rat population. I often wondered if he'd have been better left at Avery Zoo with the other feral cats, simply because of how effective a hunter he was, but then Lucky reminded me why we were supposed to be together, with a purr, or by doing something that showed me he was smarter than that. He was a cat who liked to be challenged.

"I'll take you with me to the zoo soon," I promised him. "I just don't know which way's up at the moment." Things had definitely been hectic with me running between zoos, bringing in new people, and then getting up to speed with the comic again. As if that wasn't enough, the success of *Monday's Menagerie* meant I found that I was often approached by strangers who knew who I was. That I could deal with, but it turned out they also recognised Lucky. It was my fault for drawing him accurately, but it was making me think twice about letting him loose in the zoo. He would certainly rather be out having adventures than being stroked, so he probably wouldn't appreciate too much attention. Having him on my lap was a rarity that usually demanded I drop everything and stroke him to 'encourage affection'. Beyond that, I worried that someone might take him. Fame had a strange effect on people. While I thought Lucky wouldn't go quietly, I worried about it all the same.

But I also hated leaving him behind when he liked seeing the world. Not to mention the main reason I'd started teaching him to walk on a lead and answer commands in the first place. I'd always planned that I'd continue my work as an animal welfare and breeding consultant for zoos who needed my help. I knew that before I got back to that, I had to work my magic on my own zoo, but I still liked to believe that there would come a time when I'd be able to take on consulting jobs again.

When Lucky settled down I tapped my pencil on the edge of the table and thought about everything that had happened over the past year. One year ago, would I ever have been able to imagine that I'd own my own zoo, have enough money to take on the renovation of a restaurant, and also be considered pretty famous? One year ago, I'd been saving up for a house without the thought of taking on more than my job as a zookeeper even crossing my mind.

I moved my pencil, poised to draw, but another slew of thoughts overtook me. This time, they were the familiar worries and self-doubt that come no matter how successful the outside world may consider you to be. I wondered most of all about the future of The Lucky Zoo. When the Abraham family had planned to open a zoo so close to a competitor, it had worried Avery a lot. My zoo wasn't working in competition but I couldn't help wondering if business may be negatively affected. We'd already arranged our double zoo pass deals, but there would always be some people who'd just pick one zoo, and much as I hated to admit it, that meant I would need to at least compete as much as to make sure it was an even choice. If my zoo lost out to Avery, it would be on me.

So far, it hadn't happened, but I wasn't confident about the reasons why that was the case. The dark thoughts whispered that it was only because they wanted to see the zoo owned by the comic book writer. Avery Zoo was now well-known as the zoo that had inspired the comic, and Auryn said that he'd seen a swell of business from that, but I was the person who owned The Lucky Zoo. What if that was the only reason that people were visiting my zoo, and what if it all changed the moment I slipped out of relevancy? I looked down at the blank page in front of me. I'd never felt much pressure to produce a comic that people would love, until now…

Then there was the large part of me who valued animals above all else and found it a kick in the teeth that people might be attracted to the zoo for reasons other than excellent animal care and conservation. Sometimes I just couldn't win against the voices inside.

In the end, I stomped on everything and just put pencil to paper, choosing to start with the lower pressure internet comic. My publisher would just have to keep waiting a little longer for the next volume of *Monday's Menagerie.*

I'd only managed to sketch the outline and draw one panel properly when the doorbell rang. Lucky sprang off my lap, knowing he was about to be turfed off, and then led the way to the door. It was only when I glanced out of the window on the way down the curving stairs that I remembered what Auryn had said about Timmy Marsden's brother and his wife coming to stay with us.

I pasted on a smile that was more consoling than cheery and answered the door with Lucky standing curiously by my legs. He might not always choose affection, but much like his comic counterpart, he loved sticking his nose into other people's business.

"Uh-oh," I said, just as soon as I opened the door and realised there had been a third member of the party on the doorstep. A slinky looking Weimaraner thrust forwards, making for Lucky. To my horror, I realised the dog wasn't on a leash.

In slow motion, I turned and watched as Lucky saw the big grey dog coming for him and... stood his ground. The dog sort of skidded to a halt and tilted its head questioningly. Clearly, it had met cats before, and they certainly didn't behave like this. It stuck its nose out. Lucky slapped it away with a paw and then jumped forwards. It was too much for the dog who waddled backwards, before looking up at its owners with shame written across its face.

"Sorry, we didn't know you had a cat," the man on the doorstep said.

I rather felt as though I should be the one apologising - especially when my visitor shot the dog a look that seemed to be filled with disgust.

"Lucky would face down a lion if I let him," I told them both, covering my misgivings up with another smile.

"I'm Will Marsden. This is my wife Lizzie," he said, tilting his head towards the woman next to him.

They looked nice enough. Lizzie had dark hair that fell over her shoulders in ringlets and Will had a shock of thick, dark hair, and a neatly trimmed beard. Their outfits displayed several well-known outdoors company brands, but judging by how new and neat they looked, I didn't think they'd ever been used for their intended purposes.

"And who's this?" I asked, bending down and ruffling the soft, floppy ears of the big grey dog, who looked back at me with mournful yellow eyes.

"That's Heinrich," Will informed me.

"Lovely to meet you all," I said, straightening up again. "I've got a room ready for you. If you'll follow me..." We walked up the stairs and I showed them the room with its ensuite. "Make yourselves at home. If there's anything you need, I'll be in the office working. The kitchen was just to the right of the hall we walked through downstairs. Help yourselves to anything in the fridge and cupboards."

"Thanks. I think we'll probably both grab a shower, have a snack, and then turn in. It's been a long day," Lizzie told me with a tired smile.

"How far have you come?"

"We live near Leeds, so I'm sure you can imagine the hour we got up this morning."

I nodded politely whilst simultaneously wondering how long they'd lived up there. It can't have been long enough for them to pick up the accent. They sounded like they were Surrey born and bred with their posh pronunciation.

"I'm right here if you need me," I said and then hesitated. "I'm really sorry about your brother."

They both nodded their thanks and then politely shut the bedroom door. I left them to it.

Yes, they seemed nice enough all right, but I couldn't get past the disappointed look that had been on Will Marsden's face after Heinrich hadn't gone for Lucky. What kind of dog owner wanted their pet to attack another one? And then there was the dog's name... was I being over sensitive, or had they actually named their Weimaraner after a nazi?

I bit my lip and returned to my office with Lucky back on my heels. His tail was raised high in the air to show just how pleased with himself he was feeling. I, on the other hand, was not so chipper. Auryn had agreed to have Will and Lizzie stay with us but how well did he really know them? I remembered Auryn claiming that Will had been the sensible one, whilst Timmy was the young tearaway. I wondered if that was still the case, or had times changed?

"You probably imagined it all," I said out loud, trying to convince myself that I'd never seen that look on Will's face. Anyway, I was sure they'd be gone in no time at all, and there was no doubt in my mind that Lucky was the boss dog right now.

And long shall my reign be, my plucky cat seemed to purr. Then he jumped up onto the desk and shoved a paw onto the page I'd been drawing and left a dirty smudge. I looked at it and sighed. That would take some editing out when I uploaded it! The original however... I thought about it. It was nuts, but with Lucky's added interference it would probably be worth a whole lot more than my usual original sketches. How things had changed.

Auryn called me later that evening to say he was staying over at the zoo that night. Merrylegs, the Shetland pony, was on birth watch as it was due to be her first foal and someone needed to be there at all times. The quick nature of horse birth meant that if a mare got into trouble, you had to act fast in order to save both the mare and the foal. Unfortunately, miniature horses were especially prone to complications during pregnancy. Merrylegs was currently being monitored 24 hours a day to make sure that if quick action was needed, it would be taken.

Auryn had explained that everyone on the staff had signed up for shifts so that Hayley, the current keeper at Avery who specialised in equine and other hoofed and farm animals, wasn't completely exhausted. As part of the zoo team, Auryn had signed up for the night watch. Any other time, I would have gone down there with him, but it would have been rude to leave our guests alone - especially during their time of grief.

Instead, we contented ourselves with a long conversation about life, the universe, and everything. It wasn't long before our conversation turned back to talk of the shocking discovery of Timmy Marsden's body.

"We're happy together, aren't we?" I said, voicing my sudden doubts out loud.

There was a hesitation. "Aren't you? I'm happy."

"Of course I'm happy." I sighed, knowing I was getting this all wrong. "It's just what I've been hearing recently. People seem to think cheating on their partner is part of life, something that happens all the time."

"You don't think that, do you?"

"No! I think it's terrible. I suppose I just feel stupid for assuming that people are loyal."

Auryn sounded thoughtful when he next spoke. "I think you should always think the best of people until you know for certain otherwise. Perhaps it is naive, but I like to believe that people can change if you give them a chance." He paused. "You're not worried about us?"

"I'd never consider anyone else. You're the one for me," I told him, a smile creeping onto my lips. I knew that for sure.

"I feel the same. Glad it's settled! Speaking of which... what are we going to do about our wedding? Are we still on for autumn?"

"Yes, I think we'd better," I said, sounding a little grim.

"Let's set a date. Then everything else will just fall into place, right?"

Auryn cleared his throat. "Oh, sure. Absolutely. I hear wedding planning is a piece of cake."

We shared a silent moment of amusement.

"At least we already know the venue. I'll have made it pretty and profitable by then I'm sure."

"Is profitable a key part of our wedding being planned?" I'd known Auryn wouldn't miss my jokey comment.

"You'll have to wait and see," I told him, airily.

"I think you'd better get on and open. With all of those events we've got planned for the summer, I'm certain that The Lucky Zoo will be well on its way to paying off my investment. I can't say the same for your restaurant. It's yet to make a penny, isn't it?"

I grinned. "You just wait and see! Menu planning and staff recruitment is all I've got planned for this evening. That restaurant is going to be the hottest place to eat in town."

I'd already discussed with Auryn that the restaurant should be accessible without having to go into the zoo. Obviously, a lot of the customers would probably also visit, but Auryn had agreed that it was fair and would probably help the restaurant to be seen as more than just a gimmick.

"Once you're open, I'll be the first customer. Someone's got to run the gauntlet..." he teased.

"I doubt I'll need your pity pennies," I joked back. "Anyway, I must dash, I've got important planning to do..."

When we hung up, I was smiling and felt a lot more cheerful. Auryn had been right to push me about the restaurant and our wedding planning. It was high time I got round to doing both. With a good few hours of comic creation under my belt, I set to planning out a few things I definitely wanted to see at the restaurant. My next port of call would be a fantastic chef, and then some friendly restaurant staff. I already knew that there were a few shop girls who wanted more hours, so I doubted I'd need to recruit much beyond the zoo. That was one less thing to do.

Then, there was the ace up my sleeve - Pierce Goodman. I hadn't just hired him to be my marketing and PR genius for the zoo. He was also going to be tasked with plugging the restaurant. I hoped he was as good as he thought he was.

I stood up from my desk and walked over to the window, taking a break from sitting down. The sky was dark and the moon was bright tonight, lighting up the fields that surrounded Auryn's family house. In the distance, I could see the lights of Gigglesfield, and a little to the left was the village of Lysebridge. Somewhere out amongst one of the patches of light was the small hamlet where Timmy Marsden had lived and then died. Somewhere out there a person was going about their business, knowing that they had been the one to kill him.

4

LOST DOG

I woke up the next morning to sunshine and a determination to feel cheery. The summer was in full bloom and I had a full schedule. Today I would put out ads for a chef, and then it would be over to The Lucky Zoo, before popping over to Avery to see Auryn and make sure that everything was in place for our first joint event. The arts and crafts day had been such a huge success that we'd decided to do it all again. With larger animals, like the big cats and elephants at The Lucky Zoo, I was more excited than ever to see what our participants would create.

I went downstairs to grab some breakfast and discovered a note from the Marsdens on the table. They'd gone out to walk Heinrich and were then planning to go straight to the police station.

I threw some toast into the toaster and put the kettle on. While I waited for it to boil, my mind wandered to the Marsdens and their reason for being in town. I'd done more than enough thinking about who could have done what had been inflicted upon poor Timmy Marsden, but now I wondered whose job it was to clean up the rather messy aftermath.

Seeing as there'd been no headlines about the wealthy entrepreneur behind Suck-It-In lingerie being arrested and charged with spousal murder, I assumed that Scarlett was probably free and would surely have employed someone to handle it. It wasn't as if she was short of funds.

What I couldn't get out of my head was the fate of Rameses, their pet dog. The new detective had promised to look into his whereabouts, but I'd heard nothing. Today would be the third day he'd been out, and although the weather was warm, I knew that it was unlikely he'd be finding much food. And living in a pretty rural location, his road sense was probably non-existent. I'd liked Rameses, and even though the detective had assured me it was being looked into, I was more than aware that the police would have other things to focus on.

I glanced at the clock on the kitchen wall. It probably wouldn't hurt if I put my ads out for a chef later today and made one little call first... I pulled out my mobile phone and dialled.

"Officer Kelly Lane speaking. How can I help you?"

"Hi, it's me, Madi," I said, faltering slightly. I'd called Officer Kelly before and had assumed she'd save my number. Clearly that had been presumptuous.

"Oh! Sorry about that. This new phone has decided to get rid of all of my old contacts. I'm glad you called, actually. I have a feeling you might be brought back in for a few more questions. Things aren't looking as simple as we originally thought in the Marsden case," she confided.

"Call me anytime," I said, helpfully. "I wanted to ask you something related to the case. Has anyone found the Marsdens' dog?"

There was the sound of paper being shuffled. "No, apparently some officers looked, but they couldn't find any trace of a dog."

I bit my lip, realising it was just as I feared. "It's been a few days now. I was wondering if the property is still considered a crime scene? I thought I could pop over there and have a look around to see if I can find him. It's in the interests of animal welfare," I tacked on, not wanting her to think I had any ulterior motive for going, which I genuinely didn't.

"I think cleaning is taking place this morning, so you probably don't want to get involved with any of that. I bet it will be all clear by this afternoon. However, you should contact the deceased's wife for access and to get permission. To my knowledge, she's handling all of his affairs. Or at least - her lawyer is." There was some definite resentment in Officer Kelly's voice when she said that. I'd been right to assume that Georgina Farley was a formidable lawyer.

"Okay, I'll be sure to do that," I said, walking out into the hallway when I realised the Marsdens had moved the pen I always kept on the kitchen table for note taking during phone calls.

"I hate to ask, but we're really rather stuck here. You found Timmy Marsden, right? And you knew him? Any thoughts on who might have killed him?"

"None, I'm afraid," I told her, sorry to dash her hopes. A piece of paper caught my eye on the floor and I bent down to pick it up. It was a receipt for a soy latte from Oliver's Cafe, Lyesbridge. I glanced at the time and date, vaguely registering it before I folded it in my hand.

"I was so sure that once we brought the wife in that would be it," Officer Kelly was telling me in a hushed voice. I smiled a little, pleased that she trusted me - even though I was willing to wager that the new detective would have her guts for garters if he knew.

"I'm sure some more investigation will give you an answer. There's got to be a reason behind it all," I reassured her, although I was starting to wonder... No, I had to be positive. Living in a world where people killed without even so much as a motive was just too depressing to dwell on. Whomever had killed Timmy Marsden must have had something against him. After all, hadn't the dog lead on the drive already given away that he wasn't exactly a man without enemies? "Thanks for all your help," I said before wishing the police officer a good day and hanging up.

I unfolded the receipt I'd picked up from the floor and frowned. It probably wasn't anything important, but it bothered me that I didn't know where it had come from. It was dated Sunday and the time printed was 11.10 am. Auryn and I had been getting ready to leave at that time. I'd more than likely just finished my last ever conversation with Timmy.

I thought about all of the people who'd been in the house. It could belong to Will Marsden or his wife, but they'd only come down from Leeds yesterday. I racked my brains. Who else had been by? Annabelle Wright had visited to moan about Timmy's death. Jon had been in the house, too, I realised. He'd come in to wait before giving Auryn and me a lift to the club meeting. I was willing to bet it was Jon's. He would have been on the road at that time, and it was more than feasible he'd been at the cafe close to Timmy's house.

I shrugged and tucked the receipt away. Part of me wondered why I was keeping it if I was so sure it was innocent, but another quieter voice said to keep it... just in case.

I ran a hand through my blonde hair, which was behaving itself today. If I hurried, I could pen my ad for the chef before driving over to the zoo. All thoughts of murder and my elusive house guests were firmly banished for now.

When I walked into the farm cottage at The Lucky Zoo, I

hadn't been expecting to see the look of sheer panic that crossed my newest zookeeper's face.

"How are you settling in, Gabby?" I asked her, hoping she'd come clean and tell me whatever was on her mind. She hadn't been anywhere close to this nervous when she'd come for her interview...

"Oh you know... fine."

I waited.

She cleared her throat. "There may be a slight situation, but I'm sure I can fix it. Part of the reason why I took this job was because I don't have any room for all of the chameleons I breed. I was kind of hoping I could contribute the excess to the zoo's collection. It could do with bumping up, and I have some really cool varieties!" she said, brightly.

Unfortunately, I didn't think this was the bad news...

"What's happened?" I asked, managing to keep it cool. Auryn was a natural at this kind of thing, so I was trying to take a leaf out of his book. I didn't think he would fly into a blind rage, no matter the disaster.

"Some of them escaped. They're only little, but I guess I must have not checked whether the lid was on properly. It was a new tank. I should have made sure I had it figured out. I caught most of them, but because of there being plants everywhere, even on the walls, I think there are still quite a few around. But that's not the worst part! They'd all come back to a food dish if I just waited, see? But when I came in this morning, Emma told me that a racoon had escaped. They eat everything, don't they? I asked Emma to guard the chameleons whilst I came to find you. I wanted to come clean, but..." I mentally filled in that she'd kind of hoped I wasn't going to be in today. And I also suspected that Emma had instructed her to own up, or else!

Emma, who was the zookeeper in charge of small mammals and the fowl at The Lucky Zoo, was a good employee, but sometimes a little too 'by the book'. Her standards of animal care were sky high, but I knew for a fact that her holier-than-thou attitude sometimes got up other staff members' noses.

I took a deep, calming breath. "Let me guess - the raccoon who escaped is called Billy?"

Gabby hesitated and then nodded.

"He mostly amuses himself by going through the bins, but since The Lucky Zoo is a green zoo, we've only got those recycling bins and green waste. He's probably in the green waste bin, as it's where the food will be. Baby chameleons probably aren't high on his list of things to snack on." I thought about it for a second. "Although, I wouldn't put it past him," I confessed. Some of the things I'd caught him chewing on were enough to turn your stomach. "I'll organise the hunting posse for Billy with Emma. You can go back to looking for the escapees. Then, when we've caught Billy and you've found the chameleons, I think we need to have a chat about the zoo's policies on bringing in new animals."

To be frank, there weren't any policies on bringing in animals, because I hadn't ever imagined they'd be needed. What had Gabby been thinking, adding her chameleons to the collection without asking? They could have all kinds of health problems that, without a proper quarantine, could be passed on to the current residents. Not to mention the fact that as zoo owner, I was the one who decided which animals we accepted or tried to obtain. I included the other keepers in these decisions and would have hoped they'd extend me the same courtesy.

I shook my head as I walked down the other side of the steep incline. If it weren't for the fact that I believed Gabby had her animals' best interests at heart and was also a first-rate keeper in terms of the health and welfare of the animals she bred, I'd have probably fired her on the spot. Even so, I would be making it abundantly clear that this would be her second and last chance.

"Morning, Emma," I said when the neatly turned-out zookeeper approached me down the path. The zoo was already open to visitors, but they were still in the first part of the zoo. As the responsible party for everything that went on, I would have closed the zoo if an animal that posed a danger to the public had escaped. But Billy was, well... Billy. Auryn had gifted the raccoon as a 'no hard feelings' present to the group of people in charge of setting up the then-named Mellon Zoo. We'd both known full well that he'd done it to hand over the problem of the escape artist raccoon. Now that I was the owner of the zoo, the poisoned chalice had been passed to me.

After grabbing a few passing staff members at random, I organised the search and retrieval party. When that had been done, I realised I was going to be late for my meeting with Auryn if I stayed and joined the search. With not too much regret, it must be said, I went back over to the creepy crawly house and had my talk with Gabby. Then I left everyone to it and went to attend to the event plans. With a bit of luck, Billy would be back under lock and key when the arts and crafts day happened on Saturday. Otherwise, I strongly suspected that several visitors would be losing their lunches.

When I walked up the stairs that led to the newly rebuilt and refurbished offices, I could hear laughter. As I approached, I realised it was coming from Auryn's office. The door opened as I approached and Poppy Jones, the new head of reception, walked out, mid hair-flick. I watched as she glanced coquettishly back over her shoulder before she turned and saw me.

The smile was immediately replaced with what I would have sworn was a mini-sulk before she bounced back.

"Hi Madi," she said, breezing past.

I turned and watched the blonde-bobbed woman with the annoyingly perfect curves sashay back into the main office. Then I looked back through the open door of the office at Auryn.

"You were a little late, so I was just talking through some of the plans with Poppy. She and her team have got a lot to do reception-wise on the big day. Is your team ready, too?"

"I'll be going back to them today to double check but they've been handing out flyers with every admittance and they know how to answer any questions that visitors might have about the day," I told him, keeping my voice neutral.

Auryn nodded. Was it just me, or did he look a little flushed? I bit my tongue, hard. I surely couldn't be thinking these thoughts all over again. Sure, I'd had a bit of a wobble after seeing Claudia the other day, and learning firsthand of Scarlett's less than loyal actions, but Auryn and I had talked about it. I trusted him. The voice inside whispered that while Auryn was certainly innocent of any crime, that didn't mean I had to like Poppy or her flirting.

"Let's get started then. The art supplies for children should be coming here tomorrow. Perhaps you can send someone by to pick them up? I also ordered some extra paper and pencils in case anyone who doesn't know about the event happens by and wants to take part. How have you been getting on with our keynote speakers?" Auryn asked with a lopsided grin on his face.

"Well, one of them is a bit of a diva…" I said, jokingly referring to myself, before shaking my head. "It's going fine. I need to double-check that Tiff's okay with her time slot, but all of the other local arts and crafts entrepreneurs and businesses are happy, and I think we've got the staggering of speeches worked out well, so that visitors will be able to see the things they're interested in and still have time to create their own works of art for us to judge at the end of the day. The judging panel are all sorted, too," I added. Most of the panel was made up of the speakers, having demonstrated their authority in the industry. This year, I wouldn't be on the main judging panel. Instead, Auryn and I would be picking a winner for our respective zoos.

"Sign-ups have been through the roof here. Everyone is eager to meet the best-selling author of *Monday's Menagerie*." Auryn's mouth twitched up. "You are going to have one heck of a busy day."

I nodded, smiling in return, but privately wondering how it was all going to come together. Both zoos had advertised my presence which meant I'd be doing a whole lot of running back and forth. My own speech had even been scheduled twice - once at each zoo - to allow for the predicted level of demand. The play barn was once more being used as the venue at Avery. The Lucky Zoo didn't have much by way of conference venues. In the future, I was considering potentially reconverting the Abraham family's barn conversion, so that the upstairs could be office space and downstairs would serve as a venue for times like these. As it stood, I was keeping one eye on the weather forecast and praying we'd be able to do it outdoors in the open space close to the elephant enclosure.

"I'd better go and talk to Tiff. Just so you know, our guests left to see the police this morning. They know I'll be out all day, so if they need to get back into the house, they may come here. Also, they brought a dog with them." I hoped I didn't sound too accusatory when I said that.

Auryn arched an eyebrow. "What did Lucky do to the dog?"

I laughed. Auryn knew my cat too well. "Put it this way... I think he'll be handing in his dog membership card."

We kissed each other goodbye and then I set off to find Tiff with a spring in my step. It was only when I was halfway towards the shop that I remembered I hadn't told Auryn about my zoo's escapee, or berated him for cursing me with Billy the raccoon. Sometimes his ability to be charming was sickening.

I was still smiling when I walked into the shop and greeted lots of familiar faces. Tiff saw me from where she was taking notes on stock and came over.

"Aren't the kitten Lucky toys sweet? If only they knew the truth about him now," she said. We exchanged a look. I'd told Tiff all about Lucky's thirst for blood. The dark and terrible reality would not be going into the comics, where Lucky was portrayed as a friend to all animals. "You know, you really should get a proper gift shop set up at The Lucky Zoo," Tiff said, prodding me for the umpteenth time. She was right, of course. At the moment, The Lucky Zoo had a premises that acted as a shop, but it had been built small and was fairly poorly thought out. Tiff had done what she could, but there needed to be more. I'd toyed with the idea of having gift shop stands in a kind of market area in one of the larger open spaces close to the shop.

"I thought I was going to pay you more and you'd do all that for me?" I said with a sideways smile.

Tiff waved a hand. "Oh, hush! We're friends."

"But this is business!" I protested. It was our ongoing argument. Tiff was the kind of person who'd always do something to help out a friend without expecting anything back in return. Much as I appreciated her kindness, the zoo was my business, and I wanted to treat it as such by paying people what they were worth.

Apparently I wasn't going to get my way, as Tiff changed the subject.

"I've uh... got a date tonight," she confided. Something about the way she said it clued me in that, for some reason, she wanted my approval.

"Who's the lucky guy?"

"Pierce. We had a really nice chat the other day and I gave him my number. He wants to take me to the new sushi place that's opened up in town."

"That's good, right?" I said, praying I was covering my own slight misgivings about Pierce. I'd concluded that it was simply paranoia left over from my bad experience with MI5, hadn't I?

"Yeah, it's great." She bit her lip. "Do you think he's okay?"

I knew she was asking because of Darius, her last boyfriend. I only wished I could give her a decent answer. "I know about as much as you do. His job references were good, but I've no idea what kind of a guy he is." I thought about it. "Go careful and you'll be fine."

Tiff nodded, not looking too reassured. Fortunately, the conversation then moved on to the arts and crafts day and the difficult topic of Pierce was dropped.

It was only later, when I was thinking about Pierce, that I realised Katya hadn't acknowledged my phone call or even the follow up text I'd sent afterwards to cover up the real reason I'd called her. It had only been a 'How are you doing?' text, but I had expected some kind of acknowledgement. We were supposed to be friends. All I could think to reassure myself was that Katya was deep under cover, working on a new assignment.

Something pinged in my head, reminding me that she had mentioned there could be some new developments in the case that they'd dragged me into. I wondered if it was to do with that. Fortunately, I hadn't noticed anything out of the ordinary so I was more than happy to assume that my role in all that was over. *And good riddance!* I thought, reminded of my ex-boyfriend and the two agents in their suits, whom I had grown to loathe.

Much as I liked Katya, perhaps her silence was for the best.

I was surprised to see Georgina Farley striding across the grassy picnic area when I exited the shop. I was even more startled when it became apparent that I was the person she was looking for.

"Madi! I'm so glad I found you. The nice lady officer at the station said you called this morning asking after Rameses?" The lawyer smiled broadly at me.

"I just wanted to know if he'd been found. When I discovered he was still missing, I wanted to offer to look for him myself. The police have a lot on their plates, and I'm sure Scarlett does, too," I hastily added, not wanting to make a slight against the lawyer's client.

"That's so nice of you to offer. I'm actually going over to the house myself to pick up a couple of things. Scarlett doesn't want to go back there, you see. She's also so busy with this merger. It's a real nightmare, I can tell you!" Georgina said, but the smile never fell off her face. I was starting to wonder if unnerving good humour was part of her skillset as a lawyer.

"I bet," I said, hoping I sounded like I understood half of what it was all about.

"Do you want to come with me? We can have a look for the dog. There might be a couple of questions to ask about the case, too. I wouldn't normally be so frank, but let's just say the police aren't particularly enthusiastic about having freed Scarlett. If they find anything at all that can give them grounds to bring her back in, they will. I wouldn't normally share this either, but I really don't think she did it. I'm not about to spout any guff about her loving Timmy too much, or anything like that. Put simply, she's too darn busy to bother with killing her layabout husband."

I inwardly raised my eyebrows at that description of Timmy Marsden, but to be honest, I could imagine worse. "I'll be happy to go over anything if it will help," I told her.

"Thanks, you are a star! Are you busy now? We could jump in my car and head over."

I told her that was fine and we made our way back to the car park. I happened to stick my hand into the pocket of my work trousers and felt the crumpled paper of the receipt I'd picked up from the floor that morning. "Hey, I found this in my house. It's not mine or Auryn's. Do you think it could be relevant?" I asked, showing her the paper.

Georgina looked at it and then returned it to me with a pensive look. "I'm not sure. Anything could be relevant at this point. Are you taking it to the police?"

I shrugged. "It might be nothing. I thought it was probably Jon's. He could have have passed by the cafe on his way to pick Auryn and me up. The only other people it could belong to is Annabelle Wright or Will and Lizzie Marsden - but they'd only just travelled down from Leeds yesterday."

If the lawyer was surprised or interested that Annabelle Wright had been round our house, she didn't show it. Even so, I thought I could sense she was a little intrigued, just as I was. "It's probably Jon's. I can ask him if you like? I think I have his number. He was looking over the contract at Scarlett's behest." She flicked her eyes heavenwards for a moment, showing me exactly what she thought about the rather humble solicitor examining a contract that she'd overseen.

I decided not to comment.

The rest of the journey was filled with idle chat. Georgina mentioned that she was impressed with the success of my comic and I had been suitably bashful. I'd noticed she hadn't said she was a fan - just that she was impressed by my success. I supposed I should have expected every word to be carefully considered when it came from such a high-flying lawyer.

"This whole thing is a nightmare. Nice as she is, I resent having to liaise with a police officer that I know for a fact was one of the many women Timmy had dallied with. It shouldn't be allowed," Georgina said when we were nearly at the house.

"Which police officer?" I wanted to be sure.

"I think her name is Officer Kelly." The lawyer sighed. "As I've already said, she seemed nice enough. But when I managed to get them to release Scarlett with no charge, her polite facade slipped a little. No matter how professional she may be, she's got a bias. She shouldn't be anywhere near the case!"

"Have you spoken to anyone on the police about it?"

Georgina shot me an 'are you serious?' look. "That's their job. She may be biased, but if I were to go in there and suggest they kick her off the case you can bet that would ensure suspicion was fully and firmly returned to Scarlett - jealous wife accused of murder. The less the police know about what Scarlett knew was going on, the better."

"I'm sure they've figured out enough for themselves. After all, Scarlett's alibi must have been fairly transparent. They were both at it."

Georgina nodded. "To make matters worse, Scarlett only decided to tell me right after we arrived at the station that in the long distant past she'd been carrying on with the detective, for crying out loud!"

"The new guy, Detective Gregory?" I asked, horrified that someone with such a close connection to the case was working on it.

"No, Treesden was the name she gave me. Terrible, isn't it? Whatever happened to the sanctity of marriage?"

I did my very best to keep my jaw from dropping open. I'd assumed Detective Treesden had to have been available, because Jenna had only ever been interested in men who weren't married or taken (a point that had been to her credit). All the same, Scarlett was still in her twenties, and Treesden was clearly a lot closer to retirement age than he looked - I'd give him that much. Also, I thought he was a bit of an ass, but perhaps it was a different story when you weren't suspected of a crime. I filed it as something to marvel about later.

She pulled up and we got out of the car. There was a white van parked a little further up the drive and the slogan 'From Crime Scene to Clean!' told me all I needed to know about the identity of the owner.

"They're taking their time," Georgina muttered. I'm supposed to be here to lock up after them. How about we go inside and see how they're getting on? You can take me through everything you did when you went into the house and found Timmy." She tacked the last part on so casually that it almost sounded like an afterthought. But this wasn't my first rodeo. I knew that me spilling my account to Georgina was likely to be the sole reason she'd suggested our joint excursion. Honestly, I just wished she'd be straight with me. I didn't have anything to hide from her. I'd told the police everything I'd seen and wouldn't mind doing the same for her. *Almost everything,* the voice in my head piped up, reminding me of the leather lead that was still in my handbag at home. I really had to do something about that...

When we walked in, Georgina popped through to check

on the cleaners. When she'd done that she came back to find me still standing in the hallway. It might sound crazy, but I'd needed a moment. Walking in had brought back the feeling of unspeakable dread I'd had when we'd found the door unlocked, and some sense had warned me that what lay inside was nothing good.

"So, what happened?" the lawyer asked and I forced myself to snap out of it. Timmy was dead and there was nothing to be done about that, but I was here to help - mostly for the dog, but perhaps my retelling Georgina would help reveal the person responsible for Timmy's death. Being back here could throw up some key detail I'd forgotten or overlooked.

"Auryn looked through the rooms downstairs. I think it took him a while to get to the kitchen. I went upstairs. I looked around in the bedroom. To be honest, I thought..." I trailed off. She knew exactly what I'd thought when the front door had been unlocked. "Anyway, there was nothing up there. The shower hadn't been used recently. Then Auryn called and I went back down and discovered he'd found Timmy."

"Let's go look for the dog," Georgina said with an encouraging smile, realising that I was being sucked back into the dark memory of that day. She kindly led the way back out of the front door and then in through the side gate, so that the remnants of the clean-up job wouldn't be visible.

Once outside, I focused my mind on the task at hand. "Auryn and I let him out through the patio doors. Auryn knew that there was a fence at the bottom of the garden, which theoretically kept Rameses in. But when the police were told there was a dog on the loose, they couldn't see any sign of him."

"How do you think he got out?" Georgina asked as we walked down the grassy field. "I think with all of the police around, there's a good chance he either managed to go back through the house or, more likely, someone left the side gate open. All the same, I would have thought at least someone would have remembered seeing him..." We reached the fence with its gate in the centre. "Well, the gate is closed at least, but maybe it was open when we let him out. Someone could have come up the garden..." I looked out across the thick woodland and the dirt track that led past it. The thought of the killer in the woods looking back made me shiver.

I nearly jumped out of my skin when I heard hoof-beats coming closer. There was a loud whinny. We both turned to see a large bay gelding prance around the corner, before continuing its canter towards us. I realised that the footpath was a bridle-path - as evident by the number of hoof marks on the solid mud.

"Of all the bad luck..." Georgina muttered under her breath as the rider approached.

"Gina! Whatever are you doing here?" the man on the horse called over as he drew up beside us. The large horse danced sideways and then lurched forwards. The man cursed at the horse and pulled it up. During that time, I was able to place where I'd seen him before. He'd been at The Lords of the Downs club.

"I'm here on business, Harry. I see you're not at work," the lawyer said, her voice like ice. It was the polar opposite of the unnervingly warm woman I'd been speaking to thus far.

"Oh, you know how it is. I'm cutting back on all of that these days. The company runs itself - especially now that we employ that new law firm from London," the man on the horse replied. There was something barbed about the way he said it. I looked back and forth between the two of them, trying to figure it out.

"Harry is my ex-husband," Georgina confirmed, although I had guessed as much.

"No one's good enough for our Gina," Harry added, and it wasn't said with affection.

The woman opposite me merely tightened her lips but said nothing further on the topic. Even lawyers had their limits when it came to arguments it was impossible to win.

"You're the one who came in to the club with Auryn Avery, aren't you?" Harry asked, apparently finding it preferable to address me now.

I nodded.

"Where the devil is he? Around here somewhere?" The man looked back up the field towards the house. It crossed my mind that the fence along the bottom of the garden, although a decent size, could be jumped by a horse fairly easily - especially a horse whom I assumed was bred to be a hunter.

"He's working at the zoo," I told him.

"How's he holding up? I heard he found poor old Timmy."

"He's fine." I said it with a little less decorum than I might have done if he'd included me in his sympathetic observation. I'd been there, too! *Perhaps it's a club thing to only care about other members,* I sarcastically thought.

"Who on earth would want to do the old boy in? I know he was a bit of a wild one at parties, but he wouldn't have hurt a fly!"

"Well, he was hardly innocent..." I said, goaded into saying it. "I mean, he wasn't the most faithful of husbands."

Georgina made a noise of disgust and Harry snorted in a more horse-like way than the horse he was seated on. I'd evidently hit a nerve.

"Was he definitely dallying with the ladies?" Harry pressed. "More than one? It could harm the club if something like that gets about."

"Why? He wasn't even a member. He was supposed to be inducted on the day he was murdered," I pointed out.

"Indeed. Murdered that very morning..." Harry replied. I realised that the man on the horse was a deeper thinker than I'd initially given him credit for being. That, or he'd masterminded the whole thing. I frowned and wondered if someone really could be concerned enough about the negative impact on the club's reputation to dispose of an unsuitable member. Perhaps even more than one someone...

I was still thinking about that when we all heard the sound of splashing.

"I see Ethan Pleasant is in his hot tub again. Do either of you know how the heck he has so much money? I swear he never seems to do any work," Harry commented, craning his neck to look over the hedgerow.

"You have something in common then," Georgina sniped, but it bounced straight off.

"I just want to know how he's rolling in it. I think the bounder has more cash than I do! Hullo Ethan!" he called, raising his voice.

There was the sound of more splashing and then the five bar gate between properties opened and a young man with pale skin and dark hair that hung down to his ears walked through.

"Harry, Georgina, what brings you here?" he asked the lawyer and then shut his eyes in sudden understanding. "Of course... you're working for Scarlett. I forgot you do more than just finance, you over-achiever," he said with a smile that turned his face into something appealing.

Georgina practically preened in front of Harry. "I hear you're doing very well for yourself, too, Ethan."

"Can't complain," he said with a self-deprecating shrug. "Business is as good as it's ever been. I might need to get you to look at a few more things for me. New contracts and so on. Got to make sure I'm on the right side of the law, eh?" he said, smiling all around at us.

"We're here to look for Rameses. Have you seen him around?" I asked, when the conversation seemed set to deviate into barbed words barely concealed by false pleasantries. Georgina wasn't the only one who'd taken against Harry, although having met him for all of a minute, I could definitely see why.

"The dog?" Ethan looked thoughtful. "I'm sorry, I didn't know he was missing." (I ground my teeth at that. So much for the police looking hard for him. They hadn't even bothered to ask Timmy's neighbours to keep an eye out!) "I think I heard barking down in the woods the other day, but I just assumed it was someone walking their dog. I'll let you know if I see him, and please let me know if you find him." He looked at the fence at the bottom of the garden. "Do you think he jumped over the back?"

I considered the fence a little more carefully. "It was built to keep him in. However, dogs can jump a lot higher than people think when they want to. Especially if there's something motivating them to jump."

"Do you think he went after the killer?" Ethan asked, his jaw dropping open. "That would be pretty cool!"

I shook my head. "Timmy was already dead when Rameses was let out and then went missing. The killer was long gone by then." I thought about it for a moment, wondering if I was correct to think that. Yes, Timmy had been long dead. Rameses had had blood on his side, and it had already been congealing. I didn't know the time of his death, but I assumed it had been when we'd been at the meeting and not long after I'd been on the phone to Timmy. I remembered he'd said something had come up. What was it that had distracted him?

I realised I'd zoned out and everyone was looking at me. "Sorry. It's possible he jumped the fence. If there was a female dog in heat calling, it's more than plausible that he could have cleared the obstacle and gone running off to find her. The important thing is that we find him… hopefully safe and sound." Time was already short on that front.

"I'll definitely let you know if I see him. He's a nice dog. I hope he comes back," Ethan said, inclining his head at me. All of a sudden, he frowned. "Hang on, are you Madigan Amos? I can't believe I didn't see it before! Your face is all over social media."

"It is?" I asked, feeling a little sick.

"Absolutely. You're with Auryn Avery, aren't you? He's one of the good ones," Ethan said nodding his head. I tried to smile gratefully whilst wondering about the rather strange statement. It was with some surprise that I took in Ethan again and realised he was closer to Auryn's age than mine. I couldn't help but wonder if what everything Harry had implied about him being loaded was true. He was so young to have done so much! *You're rich, too!* the little voice in my head piped up and I realised with some surprise that it was correct.

"It's terrible that this has happened. How's Scarlett holding up?" Ethan asked Georgina, continuing to rather pointedly ignore Harry.

"She's fine," Georgina said, a little too quickly. The knowledge that Scarlett Marsden was none too cut up about her husband's sudden death passed between us.

"The police asked me if I saw or heard anything on Sunday, but the whole idea of the hedgerow is for privacy. Our houses aren't even that close together. I'm not sure when it happened, but I was in the tub for some of the morning and then went out to grab some lunch." Ethan shrugged. "When I came back, the police were everywhere and I heard what had happened." The solemn mood settled upon us all for a moment. "I should be getting back. I do actually have some work to do." The sparkle in his eye clued me in that Ethan may have been listening to the conversation for longer than he'd appeared to, or perhaps he was simply well aware of the thoughts of some of the people present.

We said goodbye and then watched him go back to the other side of the hedge.

"What exactly does he do?" I asked, realising I didn't have much of a clue beyond what Auryn had said about him being a cyber whiz kid.

"He's one of those internet gurus," Harry muttered at the same time as Georgina gave a more sensible, and probably more accurate, answer.

"He offers branding and marketing advice to some significant businesses. I believe he first attracted attention by creating a slew of websites designed to compete with the businesses he was targeting. Then he beat them on the search engines and put an ad for his services on the site. It was a crazy stunt, but it got him work, and then he just went from there. I brokered a contract between Suck-It-In and his company when they used him for some marketing and search engine optimisation services. It went well, I think. That's how I know Ethan," Georgina explained. "He's a successful guy, but he has worked a lot harder for his success than some people realise."

"Can't deny he's successful," Harry said, amiably. "He's going to be in the club soon, you know. His name is next on the list and now that Timmy's gone... We like to have some diversity." The pride with which he said it made it sound like the club was giving handouts to the poor - not deigning to let in a young successful entrepreneur.

Georgina shot him a look filled with disbelief. "Your last member-to-be isn't even in the ground and you're talking about who's going to be in that stupid club! I'm going back to the house to get the things Scarlett wanted." She shot me a slightly apologetic look, but I couldn't blame her. I knew all too well what it was like dealing with an ex you would sooner strangle than chat with.

Unfortunately, that meant I was left alone with Harry.

"Ethan is a good man," Harry said, perhaps a little abashed, but about the wrong thing. "He's got his own dogs, although they're those funny sausage ones who mostly stay inside. I think he and his wife are big on stopping animal abuse, or something." His mouth twitched down when he said that. I shrewdly suspected that, quite rightly, their anti-abuse stance extended to bloodsports like fox hunting. Honestly, it was a wonder that The Lords of the Downs were even considering letting Ethan join.

"I didn't realise he was married?" I said, just to make conversation.

"Yes, she's another one of those go-getters! I think she bakes cakes, or some such. Scarlett told me one time. I think they might be good friends." My ears sharpened at his mention of Scarlett telling him 'one time'. I couldn't help but wonder if...

"I can't believe my ex-wife is getting herself mixed up in all of this nasty business, especially considering her personal involvement!"

"You mean with Scarlett Marsden's company?"

The look he gave me said that he meant something quite else. Well, well! They really were all at it.

"Perhaps it was just something to do with business," I said, neutrally.

"You know what? I wouldn't put it past Gina to be boring enough for it to be exactly that. That girl wouldn't know fun if it hit her in the face with a spade."

I looked away from Harry, hoping that lightning might strike, or the ground open up and swallow him - but leave the horse, in some strange twist of physics.

"It's good to reconnect with old Ethan. He wasn't part of

the crowd back when we were young." Harry smiled fondly at the memory. "There were always those fun tussles between our school and the local comprehensive lot. Ah, to be a kid again, eh? But it was all just a bit of fun, of course. No one really got hurt…"

I silently thought that perhaps Harry was emphasising how fun and harmless it had been a little too much. It sounded to me like there might have been some significant bullying going on. I had a strong feeling that Harry's memories of 'fun' and friendly tussles would likely be viewed as something different if I popped across the hedge and asked Ethan about his views on it. Still, perhaps times had changed - although I certainly hadn't imagined the frost between the two men.

"Hey," Ethan said, leaning back over the gate. "I think I just saw something running through the woods. It might have been a dog?"

I thanked him - perhaps a little more profusely than necessary.

"I'd better have a look," I said, inclining my head to Harry before walking through the gate at the bottom of the garden and stepping around the large horse.

"Give my best to Auryn!" Harry called before digging his heels in and making the horse jump straight from standing to canter.

I watched him go with a sour taste in my mouth. Harry seemed to believe he was fast friends with my fiancé. If he was, I would probably think a little less of Auryn - unless he gave me a very good reason otherwise.

I looked in the woods, even though I didn't really believe that Ethan had seen anything. I presumed he'd been listening to the awkward conversation over the hedge and had thankfully stepped in to save me.

It didn't take me long to see that there was no sign of any

dog in the area indicated, and after calling for Rameses a few times and then listening to the silent trees, I returned to the house, knowing there wasn't much more I could do today. Leaving the gate open and putting food out would probably attract other wildlife. I would just have to hope that Ethan would be true to his word and look out for the dog if he came home.

I really hoped he would come home.

"What else did he say about me?" Georgina asked when I walked back around the front and met her in the hallway. She was holding a pair of stilettos, which looked to be the grand sum of what Scarlett had asked her to fetch - or at least, that was all I could see.

"He implied you'd had an affair with Timmy and that you shouldn't be involved with a personal case," I said, curious enough to just say it.

Georgina rolled her eyes. "Oh, who hasn't?! Everyone has their little flings and it was ages and ages ago." She caught me looking at her and accurately read my bemusement at her hypocrisy. "Scarlett knows. We used to laugh about some of Timmy's mannerisms. It was funny."

I can't have looked convinced because Georgina laid a hand on my shoulder and made eye contact with me. "Look... Scarlett and Timmy knew what was going on. I don't know if they ever spoke about it, but they basically had an open relationship. They still loved each other, but they saw other people, too. Just... sometimes the people they saw might not have understood that. They were never serious with anyone else, you see."

"Okay," I said, once more trying to sound neutral. I felt like I'd dropped into a parallel universe these past few days.

"By the way, Scarlett said you told her to avoid using her personal lawyer. Was there a particular reason for that, or was it just 'the usual'?"

"I'm certain she was involved with Timmy," I told her, thinking dark thoughts about our doorstep encounter. "But the real reason was that she might have been at the house that morning. I know her husband was..."

"Her husband?"

I blinked and realised I hadn't shared anything about the dog lead I'd found with her. It had stayed between the three of us - Auryn, Jon, and I.

"He left a dog lead that had been given to him by Timmy on the drive. I'm assuming that he was the one who left it," I confessed, hating myself for gossiping.

"Interesting. The police don't know?"

"No. I was going to talk to Andy Wright about it. Auryn thought that a woman visiting him might be less likely to incur a poor reaction..." I hoped that didn't sound too much like I suspected Andy Wright of being the killer. I'd met the man at the barbecue and wouldn't have thought he'd have it in him. But people had done crazier things in the name of love...

"I could come with you when you go?"

"I'll let you know," I said, unwilling to commit. I was finding I enjoyed the lawyer's company for the most part, but there had definitely been something alarming about the way her personality had taken a flying leap into psycho when her ex-husband had turned up. I supposed that potentially wasn't the most abnormal reaction in the world, but it still made me a lot less inclined to trust Georgina Farley.

There was the sound of something hitting the floor upstairs. We both turned to look up and then, as one, we crept up the staircase. Somehow, I'd ended up leading the way, and it was only when I was a couple of steps away from the landing that I considered what might lie at the top. My first thought had been that Rameses must have come back home and somehow slipped inside, but what if the truth was a lot more dangerous? The killer could have come back for something.

I stepped into the bedroom and drew in a sharp breath.

"Window's open a bit. I think a breeze blew over that picture frame by the look of things," Georgina said and then looked at my expression. "Are you okay?"

"Someone's trashed this room. It didn't look anything like this when I came up here on the day of the murder!"

5

MERRYLEGS

"Are you sure?" Georgina asked, looking around with more interest. "Perhaps the police disturbed a few things in their search. But it is rather unlikely that they would cause such a mess. I'll have to ask them."

I nodded, taking in the room more carefully. Scarlett had a sizeable selection of perfumes, and their original boxes had been stacked up on the dressing table, I recalled. Now they were all over the floor and most were lying open. *They were looking for something small,* my brain supplied. I wondered if they'd found it.

Georgina reassured me she'd contact the police and we left the house. I left the receipt with Georgina when she returned me to Avery Zoo. She'd promised to ask Jon if it belonged to him, and I thought it best that it was left with someone whom I assumed wouldn't be as likely to lose it as I was. My new accountant had nearly broken down when I'd brought my tax return for him to do last month - and that had just been for my consulting work for the most part, as my comic hadn't taken off back then. With the zoo and the comic added into the mix this year, I thought it more than likely that come next year, I was going to be all accountants' public enemy number one.

I was intercepted by the police before I made it through the entrance. The new detective, Alex Gregory, was leading the group and I recognised Officer Kelly as one of the other two police members accompanying him.

"Is everything all right?" I asked, concerned that something had happened at the zoo since I'd been gone.

"It's important that we ask a few further questions regarding the death of Timmy Marsden," Detective Gregory began.

"I'll do all I can to help," I assured him, eager to repair any damage caused at the police station when Treesden had still been sneaking around.

"Did you see anything that might have been the murder weapon when you were present at the scene?"

I pricked my ears up at the mention of murder. It had been fairly obvious that Timmy Marsden hadn't slipped and fallen or even done himself in, but all the same, no one had officially confirmed it prior to now.

"I'm afraid I didn't see anything that might have done it. It looked like a knife wound. I assumed he was stabbed," I told him.

"Madi! Great, you're here. You've got to come and see the new foal. Merrylegs has literally just given birth!" Tiff's voice floated out from reception as she dodged visitors and rushed out to the car park, her strawberry blond hair flew out behind her and her face was flushed with excitement. Tiff was the only person I knew who looked beautiful whilst running. Her running was never fast, but boy, was it glamorous.

"Sorry! I didn't realise you were in the middle of something," she said when she arrived, coming to a stop and flashing a breathtaking smile at the police present.

For the second time in two days I watched the sparks fly. This time it was Detective Alex Gregory who had just fallen head over heels for my best friend. As plot twists went, it was an interesting one.

The detective turned around and instructed his accompanying staff to head back to the police station, as there were apparently only a few loose ends to tie up. Then he amusingly suggested we all take a trip to see the new foal.

It was the first time during an interview with the police that my interviewer had actively been keen to let me go as soon as possible. When I walked away from the Shetland pony enclosure, I turned and flashed a smile at Tiff from behind the detective's back. She slightly raised her eyebrows in return, and I knew that although she was keeping her cool, she was equally interested in the new detective. I walked away wondering what would become of it all. She'd been singing praises to Pierce, but now there was a new man on the scene... who would she pick?

I smiled at this slice of normality. Tiff had often been beset by offers. I'd always been the one to listen to the pros and cons of each and then have nights of discussion in front of the TV with a bucket of popcorn between us. Feeling nostalgic, I made a mental note to schedule one of those nights with Tiff soon. You should never be too busy to spend a girly evening with your best friend.

I met up with Tiff again later and she confided everything I had already known about her and the new detective on the force. Unsurprisingly, he'd already asked her on a date.

"I just feel like I've been really naive. Is everyone really cheating on everyone else?" I asked, when the conversation moved on to the now-confirmed murder.

"I don't know why you're focusing on that. If I were you, I'd be huddled in a corner right now because I saw a corpse," my best friend said.

"Well, it's not as if it's my first one."

"Quite," Tiff replied, and I felt like there might have been some point I'd missed. "You're not really worried about Auryn, are you?"

"No, of course not," but my voice lacked conviction even to my ears. "It's not Auryn, it's other people. I'm sure she's nice, but the new head of reception looked really friendly with him when I saw her coming out of his office."

"Oh, Madi! Please tell me you aren't turning into a jealousy monster?"

"I'm not! Am I?" I bit my lip. "I do trust Auryn. Of course I do." I was certain of that.

"Good. Then you shouldn't think anymore on it," Tiff said with such hotness that I felt my cheeks flush with embarrassment.

Tiff followed her reprimand up with a smile and I knew the matter had been dropped. "I think I'm going out for a drink with Alex tonight. You'll be there as my emergency text contact, won't you?"

It took me a second to realise she was talking about the detective. First name terms already! "Of course I will be, although, he is the law, so you shouldn't have any trouble. Or if you do, I probably can't get you out of it without being arrested."

Tiff rolled her eyes and grinned. "You're so reassuring. Anyway, he seemed nice. Perhaps he's a good man."

"Perhaps," I echoed, not wanting to colour her opinion in any way. My own bumpy start with the detective was not entirely guiltless on my part. I hoped that Tiff would see a different side of the new detective, and who knew what might come of it? At the very least, I was hoping she'd put in a good word or two on my behalf. With my track record, I might need it.

———

After sorting a few organisational things out for the forth-coming event and spending some more time admiring the new piebald foal, I returned to The Lucky Zoo to discover what had become of the lost chameleons and the devious raccoon. To my relief, Billy was back inside his enclosure and the pile of rocks and food debris he'd been subtly piling up in order to facilitate his escape had been removed. His keepers were under strict instructions to look out for his tricks in the future. I didn't for a second think that it would be the last time Billy escaped, but it wouldn't be for lack of trying on our part.

The chameleons had come back to their food bowl of crickets and had then been returned to the tank. According to Gabby, they were still young enough to share but would soon need to be separated out. When I asked her what we were going to do with so many chameleons, she'd asked politely if the zoo might consider becoming a renowned breeder of chameleons, as it was her speciality. I'd told her I would think about it, seeing as she'd asked me. Although I was keen to not appear too pleased with the keeper who'd gone behind my back, the idea certainly appealed to me. I'd already decided that I would contact Snidely Safari - a zoo I'd consulted for, who had a world famous collection of reptiles and amphibians - and ask their advice on how to put the word about. I was determined that The Lucky Zoo would not be isolated and would instead become a helpful part of the conservation efforts of zoos across the country.

I did the evening round, checking that everything was as it should be. My walk took me on the long trek around the elephant enclosure, and I was pleased to see that Donald Trunk and his family were showing healthy elephant behaviours. I watched the bull elephant fan his ears and wondered if in the future the zoo might be fortunate enough to have a baby elephant. With a 22 month gestation period after mating, I knew that it was a hope I'd have to hold onto for a while to come.

My mind drifted back to the Marsden house and the destruction in the bedroom. For some reason, my mind danced back to the late Jenna Leary and her bad habit of hiding things on memory cards and in print in order to get her own way. I wouldn't have called it blackmail, as her goals had never truly been malicious, but it certainly hadn't been honourable either. I wondered if Timmy had shared that trait.

On the topic of infidelity, I was pleased that Detective Treesden had retired just as the case got underway. Now that I knew his prior involvement, it was surely a good thing that he was remaining clear of a case where he had strong ties with the person who was probably still suspect number one. The same could be said for Officer Kelly, who was still on the case, but I hoped she'd be able to decide whether or not she was in too deep.

I made a determined effort and shut the lid on the murder investigation. I had enough on my plate to be getting on with, including making amends. I'd thought about the conversation I'd had with Tiff and now I pulled out my phone, composing an 'I'm sorry I've been a bit crazy' text to send to Auryn. I would have to think of something to make it up to him if I'd been as bad as Tiff had implied.

I really hoped it would be the last time I'd need to send a text to my husband-to-be because of my own overactive imagination.

By the time I'd finished my round, I'd made the decision to swing by Avery Zoo to catch Auryn at the end of the day. I went bearing the gift of takeaway dinner, as I knew Auryn well enough to suspect that his current heavy workload would mean he wasn't eating well. There'd been a time when Auryn had looked like a surfer who worked out on the side. These days, he appeared as lean as a model, but not necessarily in a good way. He was still getting the workouts in, but sometimes he just forgot to eat. There were times when I wished I could have a few days of that myself...

"I'm sorry about... everything," I said, once we were sat down in the open square between the otter and beaver enclosures. The zoo was empty of people but the evening was still light.

"I was never worried," my fiancé told me with a smile. "We've been under a lot of stress, and finding out about other peoples' dirty laundry can make you doubt those who are around you. Plus, we saw someone who had died in a terrible way. It does have an effect, you know." The last part seemed almost like a gentle jibe.

"It's your first one," I suddenly realised, thinking about the number of times I'd had the misfortune to come across corpses and then Auryn's comparative inexperience.

"I'm surprised you're as well-adjusted as you are," Auryn told me.

"Try not to think about it too much," I said, feeling my mind disobey me the instant I said it. Images of a surprising number of bodies and their diverse causes of death assailed me for a moment. I shook them away.

"I'll just be glad when it's all over," I added.

Auryn nodded. "I just hope it was none of my friends who were responsible, but I know how it looks..."

"That reminds me..." I said and then told him about meeting with Georgina Farley's ex-husband Harry, and then Timmy's next door neighbour, Ethan.

"Hmmm Harry... what did you make of him?"

I found I only needed four words to describe him.

"That sounds about right," Auryn concurred with a smirk. "Back at Harvington House he was always a bit full of himself. He was sixth form age when I was just starting. Was he in the garden at the same time as Ethan?"

"Yes, and it wasn't exactly comfortable."

"Ethan's a good guy. You probably noticed we're close in age. He's done well for himself. I'd prefer him over Harry any day."

"But Harry said you were such good friends!" I teased, making Auryn groan.

"I think someone might have broken into the house since the murder," I told him, and then explained what I'd seen and my theory about the size of what had been searched for. "There weren't any signs of a break-in, but who knows if the house really was locked up before we got there? All it would have taken was the police to forget locking the back door. There's all that land leading up to the property. Ethan probably wouldn't notice because the hedge is so high."

"Do you think they found what they were looking for?" Auryn asked. I shrugged. There was no way to know for sure.

"Harry accused Georgina of being involved with Timmy. I thought Scarlett would have picked a lawyer who wasn't involved with her husband. You'd think they'd be worst enemies!" I bit my tongue when I realised I was dangerously close to revisiting a familiar topic.

"Other people have other views," Auryn told me with an understanding smile. I smiled back and we looked up at the first few stars appearing against the fading sky.

We arrived home to find we had the house to ourselves. There was no note to suggest that Will and Lizzie Marsden had returned, so they must be staying out for dinner. We had the house to ourselves and I suggested we made good use of it. It was only later when I was about to go to sleep that I reflected that in spite of a murder and the combined busy-ness of our two zoos, we still had more time to spend together now than we had when we'd gone on holiday. I smiled at the darkness and said a silent prayer of thanks that - all things considered - the world had been pretty good to me.

6

FOLLOWING A LEAD

I woke to find a text from Tiff recounting every detail of her drinks date with Alex Gregory. It had apparently turned into a full-blown night out, and she'd only got back in the early hours. I spared a thought to wonder if the detective thought it wise, considering he was currently in charge of a murder investigation. But then, Tiff had her own job to do, too. I thought they'd probably just been having too good of a time to care. A sudden thought of a double date popped into my head. I laughed out loud before I could stop myself.

Auryn turned to look at me.

"Just warming up for my big speech," I told him with a raised eyebrow. Today I was due to give a pep talk to the entire staff of The Lucky Zoo about the arts and crafts day that was taking place on Saturday. It was the first time I would be addressing everyone I'd employed, and I was definitely feeling the pressure. I'd got to know everyone who worked for the zoo pretty well, but I needed to encourage them to go out and get 'em on the arts and crafts day to make sure it was a roaring success. I had run a few thoughts by

Auryn and then asked his advice. Unhelpfully, he'd told me to go out and start talking and that it would all turn out great. I thought that probably rung true for him, but I didn't have that unlearnable spark of charisma he definitely possessed. *Hopefully it won't be a car crash,* I thought, turning my head to look out of the window to see what the weather was doing today. A face popped up and I cried out in dismay.

"What? Oh," Auryn finished, once he'd turned and looked out of the window, too. "We're two floors up. How is he on the windowsill? And with half a dead rabbit. Where did the other half go?"

I decided to answer the least grisly question. Anyway, Auryn was well aware that Lucky had decided to supplement his diet. "I think the wisteria might be a little out of hand if it's thick enough for him to climb all the way up here. Maybe we should do some gardening?"

"That would be nice. Of course, we don't tend to have a lot of free time, but maybe once this event is done, we could take a couple of days? Get some wedding planning done, too?" He nudged me in the ribs.

"It would be nice."

"Annabelle Wright is coming in to talk to me about the latest event regulations and how they affect financial law, or something incredibly dry along those lines," Auryn said, changing the subject.

"Maybe you can ask her why the dog lead given to her husband was on Timmy Marsden's drive on the day of his death."

"Maybe I can, although, you're not seriously thinking he did it, are you? A crime historian would surely know better than to leave a glaring clue revealing his own identity at the scene of the murder. Especially given his speciality…"

I shook my head when he tilted his head at me. I'd seen the lead get passed over with great aplomb at the barbecue, but I hadn't actually spoken to the mousey man who'd received it. I thought it was high time I made my own judgement on whether or not Andy Wright was capable of murder.

My pep talk went much better than I'd predicted. The outside area behind the barn, which wasn't open to the public, had definitely felt like an uplifting place to be once I'd finished. I'd still been congratulating myself when Pierce had tapped me on the shoulder.

"How has progress been?" I asked with a smile. I'd managed to pin Pierce down over email as to a few of his concrete plans for the zoo beyond 'wait and see what I can do'. They'd seemed solid and legal. If they worked, then that would be exactly the result I was hoping for.

"Everything's going to plan," he said, somehow managing to make it sound like we were planning a presidential assassination. I hoped Donald Trunk's large ears weren't flapping.

Pierce shifted from foot to foot and looked nervous for the first time since we'd met. "Has, uh, your friend mentioned me at all?"

"She told me you went out on a date the same day you met," I said, neutrally.

He nodded. "Yeah, I thought it went well. I was going to follow up today." Something about the way he said 'follow up' made me hesitate.

"Are you going to ask her out again?"

"I'll text her and see how she is," he said, in a vague way that made me wonder even further. Was he a part of the 'treat them mean to keep them keen' brigade? If he was, then I would be telling Tiff to ditch him in a heartbeat. However, I was willing to cut him some slack if it turned out that for all his charm and shine, Tiff had made him go to pieces. It wouldn't be the first time she'd had that effect on a man. *Or the last,* my brain added.

I decided to visit the creepy crawly house after I'd finished with Pierce. Gabby was nowhere to be seen, but I'd wanted some time to check out what she'd been up to while she was away working on something else - especially after the bumpy start we'd had.

I peered into the enclosures I'd overseen when the zoo had first been set up and was pleased to see that changes had already been made. I'd always known that reptiles and amphibians weren't my speciality, so everything I knew was secondhand information. So far, the things that Gabby had added and taken away from the vivariums and enclosures looked to be improvements - although I was sure time and the results in the health of the animals would tell for sure. Even so, I was pleased. I'd wanted someone who would be able to put their own stamp on the creepy crawly residents at The Lucky Zoo, and so far, I was pleased.

I halted next to a tank that was fairly teeming with tiny chameleons. Gabby had explained they were veiled chameleons and were only a week old. To my eyes, there looked to be as many as a hundred in the vivarium. She'd explained that in a day or two, they'd need to be sorted according to size. The smaller chameleons would be around 1.2 grams in weight, whilst the larger hatchlings could be 1.5 grams or more. Separating them ensured the health of all the chameleons, as the slower developers wouldn't lose out to their larger peers.

I spared a thought as I watched a tiny chameleon tangle with another equally tiny chameleon to wonder about the way we subverted the laws of nature for our own ends. I shook my head. You always had to keep conservation in mind. We were always working to promote conservation both through breeding and through making animals visible and accessible to visitors, in order to help their wild cousins survive. However, I knew the distinction between natural selection and helping animals in need got a lot more complicated when you were working with actual wildlife. I was glad that I never had to make those kinds of decisions in my line of work. *Anyway, Lucky makes most of those choices for you,* I thought, darkly.

Speaking of dark thoughts, I had something else scheduled in for the rest of the morning...

It hadn't been all that hard to think of an excuse for meeting Andy Wright and get him to agree to it. I'd arranged the meeting under the guise of putting together an event for local writers to engage with local readers. I'd actually been pretty pleased with the idea and would have genuinely considered it, had I not possessed the strong suspicion that Andy Wright was unlikely to want to see me again after we'd had our meeting.

The man who answered the door was in his late thirties. He had pleasant mouse-brown hair and a face that was friendly, but forgettable. If someone had asked me to describe him to a police sketch artist, I wasn't sure I'd be able to. The dark brown and white flecked dog by his side, who looked up with soulful hazel eyes, was far more memorable.

"Madigan Amos! I've been trying for years to do what you seem to have accomplished in five minutes," Andy Wright said, thrusting out a hand and shaking mine in a rather limp manner.

"Well, I have been working at it for rather longer than that. You know what they say about being an overnight success... that it can take a lifetime of work to achieve," I said good-naturedly. All the same, I couldn't help being a little put-out. I was well aware that the success I'd gained, seemingly in a short amount of time, was more than many writers ever dreamt of achieving in their whole career, but I'd hoped that another author would sympathise, not share the view of the masses.

"I think we nearly met a couple of weeks ago at a barbecue?" I said when Andy had invited me inside the house.

"Oh yes?" he asked, gesturing that I could pick a chair.

"The one at the Marsdens' house." I kept my voice neutral. Andy had his back turned to me, but I noticed it stiffened when I mentioned the Marsden place.

"I don't know how I missed getting an introduction. I suppose Annabelle and I did make it a flying visit. I'm sure you were all anyone was talking about," he said, turning and giving me a polite smile.

"I very much doubt that," I told him, thinking of the huddles and whispering that had gone on - the same as I'd witnessed at the club. The members of The Lords of the Downs had been far more wrapped up in themselves than the little old comic book writer in their midst. "Was there any reason why you and Annabelle didn't stay? It was such a lovely day." Perhaps I was laying it on a bit thick, but I wanted Andy to come clean of his own accord.

"Oh, you know… we're both busy people."

I gave up and pulled out the hand-tooled leather lead I'd popped into my handbag on the day of the murder. Andy Wright looked at it warily, as if it were a particularly dangerous snake that might spring to life and bite him at any time. "I was wondering when that might turn up," was all he said.

"I found it before I found Timmy. I picked it up before I knew what had happened to him. Then, Jon, Auryn, and I thought we'd ask you about it before sharing something like that with the police. We saw no reason to drag an honest man's name through the mud," I said, hoping I looked suitably apologetic.

The writer kept his eyes on the dog lead. "You should have given it to the police."

I waited.

"I didn't kill him," he finally said after a long pause. He sighed and sat back, spreading his hands wide on the arms of the chair. "I love my wife. I really do. I thought Timmy was a good friend, and I am sorry he's dead. I found out that my wife was having an affair with him on what turned out to be the day he died. I went over there that morning to have it out with him and tell him to keep his hands off! But when I arrived, I bottled it." He looked down at the ground. "I could hear his dog barking at something and someone was playing a radio really loudly out the back. I thought there was some shouting over it, too, but it could have just been the music." He ran a hand through his hair. "Looking back, knowing what I know now, maybe I heard the killer. I threw the lead down and left, telling myself it would send as good a message as any." He sighed. "I just can't get it out of my head. I let myself be put off by classic rock and a dog. It probably would have taken less. I just don't have the backbone needed. That's probably why she went off in the first place..."

"Nonsense!" I said, stepping in. "False bravado definitely doesn't make the man. If Annabelle has decided to go off with someone else, it's her choice to do wrong by you. If she's not happy about something in your marriage, she should have talked to you, not shacked up with your friend." I bit my lip and then decided to ask. "Why was it that Timmy was giving you the lead as a present?" I thought I knew the reason, but I couldn't quite remember...

"Oh, that's simple. Annabelle and I looked after Rameses when Timmy was off in Nepal. Apparently Scarlett was too busy to be tied down with caring for him. It's usually the same with our German Shorthaired Pointer, Napoleon - I'm in charge of keeping him whilst Annabelle funds our lifestyle. It's something I've been reminded of a lot lately."

"That sounds like something you need to talk to her about." I was starting to feel a lot like a marriage counsellor.

He nodded. "Probably. Writing doesn't pay as well as it used to, you know..." he said, and then looked pained when he remembered who he was talking to.

"I should go to the police about what I heard. The killer hasn't been found have they?" He looked hopeful.

"Not yet. I suppose we've both done wrong, covering up what we knew. How about we both come clean together?" The crime historian nodded.

We made the call to the police station, confessing to our joint avoidance of civil duty. It wasn't long before the phone was handed over to Detective Gregory, but while he was none too pleased, and demanded to see the dog lead in question and Andy Wright, he was a lot less explosive than I'd feared. I strongly suspected that I had Tiff's influence to thank for that. In turn, I silently made note to tell my friend of the detective's good deed.

At the end of the conversation, the detective asked to speak to me again. Andy handed over the phone with a solemn look that I did my best to echo.

"I hope you know I am doing you a favour. What you've done is extremely irresponsible, not to mention stupid." The hushed tones he spoke in let me know he was doing his best on his side to not let the conversation be overheard. "You're the name on everyone's lips at the moment. It would be well within my power to bring you in for obstruction of justice, and what would that do for your reputation?" *Probably wonders,* I privately thought, remembering the antics of my short-lived stint with a publicist. He'd have probably actively encouraged perverting the course of justice in order to get a great headline and a photo op.

"Thank you. I do know you're doing me a favour and I appreciate it. I'm sorry," I added, hoping I was conveying that I really did regret how this had turned out. I'd realised since confronting Andy that I'd hoped there was some other explanation as to how the lead had ended up on the drive. In fact, I'd actually hoped that it had been a second similar lead, perhaps brought back from Nepal for Rameses. Beyond that, I'd just wanted to give Andy Wright the chance I'd never been given to have a say before being dragged in for questioning.

"Thank you for introducing me to your friend," Detective Gregory added in an even quieter voice.

"Not a problem." Now it was my turn to lower my voice and move away from listening ears. "I know she had a nice time," I told him, throwing him a bone before saying goodbye.

I handed over the lead to Andy Wright. Then I left him at the mercy of the Gigglesfield police force.

I'd planned to devote the next day to working on my comic. The main reason for that was that my publishers were due to come down on Saturday. They were coming to visit the arts and crafts day as special guests and to review the progress I'd made.

I was determined that there would actually be some progress for them to review.

Will and Lizzie Marsden breezed in and then out that morning with barely a hello. I understood that they were distraught by the loss of a close family member, and were also tasked with organising a funeral, but I had expected a little more from Auryn and my guests. Even their Weimaraner had been snooty ever since having his run in with Lucky.

I turned to the cat himself and shrugged, before finishing my orange juice. There was a long day of drawing ahead of me. I was glad when he followed me upstairs and then settled down on the sofa on the other side of the office. I liked to warm up before sketching and Lucky always made a great life model. A rather sedentary one when he was curled up, but I always liked to draw him even if it was just to marvel again at how much he'd changed since I'd rescued him from abandonment by his mother.

"Your siblings are doing well, although, I think you outsize them all these days," I told the already snoring cat. "You were just a late starter."

I picked my mechanical pencil up along with my practice sketchbook and then it was down to work.

A few hours later, my focus was broken by the house phone ringing. I didn't usually answer it, as it either wasn't for me, or was a junk call, but too much time spent glued to a piece of paper meant I was desperate for a break.

"Hello?" I answered the phone.

"Madi, is that you? It's Georgina Farley. I don't have a number for you, I'm afraid. We really should have swapped the last time we were together. Anyway, listen…" she said, getting to the meat of why she'd called. "…I was wondering if you might be willing to go over a few more things. Scarlett really is worried about how no one seems to be doing anything to solve this awful murder. I know there's probably nothing more you can tell me, but it will make her happy. I thought we might check out Oliver's Cafe."

"Okay, I could be there in fifteen minutes, if you're near-by?" I said and we agreed on the time.

When I hung up I raised my eyebrows. Either Georgina

was using the cafe as a dangled carrot to pique my curiosity, or she believed there might be something more to that abandoned receipt I'd found on the floor of the hallway.

Whatever her reason was, I was both intrigued enough and stiff enough from too much time spent hunched over my desk, to go to the cafe.

Who knew? It could be a lead in the case. And if there was anything at all criminal, I would tell the police sooner rather than later, because I had definitely learnt my lesson.

Probably definitely.

Oliver's Cafe was one of those nice homespun cafes. There weren't the rugged brick walls or slick canvases showing coffee growers in South America that the large faceless chains always seemed to possess. Instead, there was pinstripe wallpaper and an eclectic mishmash of furniture that reminded me of a particularly cosy jumble sale.

Georgina waved me over and we approached the counter together.

"I wonder if you can help us?" Georgina said, pulling out the rather battered looking receipt. "Were you working here at the time and date shown? We just want to find out if you remember anything." Her smile was charming and disarming, but it was also totally ignored. That was because the young man behind the counter was staring at me.

"You're famous! I can't believe you're in here. Someone said you were a local and ran a zoo, but I thought they were joking. Can I have your autograph?"

I didn't have to look for a reflective surface to know that I was blushing. It always happened when I got caught by surprise. "Of course! I'll be happy to. While I sign something, would you mind having a look at the receipt?"

"Sure!" the young man said, seizing it from Georgina's hand and making a good show of scrutinising it. I found a clean paper napkin and borrowed a pen from behind the counter.

"Oh yeah, I was working at that time. It's busy then. Do you know who it might have been?" He looked over my shoulder at the tiny drawing of Lucky I was doing on the napkin. "Awesome," he breathed. I spared a hope that this wouldn't end up on eBay as soon as the server's shift ended.

"It might have been a man with thinning brown hair and pale skin, who was dressed in a suit. He has a mole on his cheek," I said, describing Jon."

"Or maybe a smartly dressed woman with auburn hair that was probably pulled back into a bun," Georgina piped up.

The server frowned with concentration. I decided to have a final, unlikely punt.

"It could have been a couple. A man with dark hair and a beard. Medium build, but a little on the pudgy side. He would have been with a woman who had dark hair that's got ringlets to here," I moved a hand near my shoulder. "She's slim and..." I searched for something more specific and then remembered the couples strange preference for professional outdoor gear. "They both might have been wearing outdoorsy stuff, only they don't look very outdoorsy."

To my intense surprise, the man's eyes lit up. "Oh yeah! I saw the woman in here, just like you described. That's so weird, I remember thinking 'there's no way you've ever climbed Everest," he told us with a grin.

"You're sure?" I asked.

"Yeah, totally. Oh, I think the first guy you described is a regular here." He frowned. "Jon, I think his name is? He's a nice guy. He didn't come in on that morning though."

"Thanks for your time," Georgina said, taking the receipt back and smiling thinly at him.

The server didn't even notice the shade she threw at him. He was too busy admiring the scribbled-on napkin. "Thanks a mill!" he said before running over to another server to show them my less than perfect handiwork.

"That'll be on eBay before the hour's up," my companion grumbled uncharitably. Sure - I'd been thinking the same thing, but I hadn't actually said it.

"What on earth was Lizzie Marsden doing in a cafe so close to Timmy's house on the day that he was killed?" Georgina mused the second we were outside the door.

I looked back at the cafe for a second, wistfully noting that we hadn't even grabbed a takeaway drink. "I have no idea. She was supposed to be in Leeds. That's where her husband said they were prior to coming all the way down here."

The lawyer and I exchanged a long look. I knew we were both wondering the same thing. Had Lizzie Marsden been having a very long distance affair with her brother-in-law? "Honestly, it's getting to be a farce," I muttered, referring to the number of extramarital affairs that had been going on. Amongst the selection of estranged partners and disgruntled spouses it was a wonder that both Timmy and Scarlett hadn't been bumped off long ago - or even tried to do the same to one another. *Unless Scarlett finally snapped,* I silently reminded myself. But why would she have snapped now of all times, when it was clear that Timmy had been carrying on quite openly for years?

"Lizzie's still at your house, isn't she? You need to ask her what she was doing down here," Georgina told me.

"It could be a false ID. I suggested what she was wearing and a few vague features. It wasn't the best description ever..."

"Find out a good way to ask her... so she won't just lie." Georgina tapped her chin with two fingers. "You know... they may be a small cafe, but they sure have invested in their CCTV system. Did you notice it was top of the range? Must be a sign of the times..."

"Really? Then why didn't we just ask to see..." I trailed off when I realised what she'd done. We'd only just left the cafe and I'd been ready to believe that there'd been a CCTV system I hadn't noticed. Would the same trick work on Lizzie Marsden? I thought there was a chance it just might.

I hadn't been overly keen on the pair staying at the house in the first place... but harbouring a killer was quite another matter. And if Lizzie Marsden really had been at Oliver's Cafe at the time indicated on the receipt, it would put her firmly in the time frame for committing a murder.

7

CAT-EAT-DOG

I got back to find Auryn was at the house.

"There you are! I thought you were doing comic stuff all day?"

"I got a lot done," I said, rather defensively. "I decided to take a break, so I went out for coffee with Georgina." *Coffee we'd never actually had*, I recalled again, miserably. "Are the Marsdens back yet? There's something I need to ask Lizzie."

"Uh, no, actually. Will texted me to say they're going to be leaving this evening. I think they've had enough. It's probably finally hitting home for them." Auryn sat down at the kitchen table and reached for the bowl of cereal he'd poured himself. It was past lunchtime, but I knew from experience that Auryn would quite happily eat cereal for all three meals of the day if given the opportunity.

"What about the funeral?" I asked, sitting down and stealing a sugar puff. I pulled a face a moment later. Why would anyone ever pick a cereal that tasted soggy to start with?!

"Will said in his text that the police were vague about when the body might be released for burial. I think now they've been given a concrete answer. I can only assume that it must not be for a while."

"Do you know where they are now?"

Auryn frowned. "You're asking a lot of questions about them all of a sudden. I'd got the impression they weren't your cup of tea."

"Only because they aren't exactly friendly." I hesitated. "Not that I really blame them, I suppose. They're not here to be sociable."

"So, why the questions?"

I quickly explained about my mini investigation with Georgina and the surprising results it had yielded. I made sure I included my misgivings about how reliable our source had been.

"If it's true, then that's something we should go to the police with," Auryn commented.

I nodded emphatically. "But we don't know it's true yet. At the moment it's nothing more than gossip. I don't want the police to think I'm some nosy gossiper."

Auryn raised one eyebrow and then the other one.

"Hey!!" I protested. "I'm just inquisitive."

"Almost to a fault," my darling fiancé informed me. "However, as a courtesy, it might be good to find out for ourselves before handing it over to the authorities." There was a glitter to his eyes when he said it.

"A courtesy to whom?"

"Timmy, of course. We owe it to him to get the truth out of Lizzie and Will, if they really were in the area at the time of the murder and have neglected to mention it to anyone."

"The server only said he saw Lizzie."

"Will could have been outside waiting in the car. Or perhaps it was Lizzie on her own," Auryn said with a shrug.

"Or perhaps it wasn't her at all," I added, playing devil's advocate.

"Well, we'll find out when they come back to collect their stuff later on. We'll just make sure we're both around… in case of adventure." He threw me a sideways smile and then raised his eyebrows again. "Shouldn't you be drawing?"

I shot him a hurt look and exited the room. How dare he know I was doing everything within my power to procrastinate? I spared a smile when I walked back into the office and sat behind my desk. I'd heard that some writers' houses were spotless because they cleaned when they were trying to avoid writing. In my case, the house stayed messy, but the fridge experienced a good clean out.

When my stomach grumbled, I looked up and discovered it was nine o' clock at night! Caught in a slight panic, I stuck my head out of the office and then stalked down the corridor to the guest room.

The Marsdens' stuff was still there.

"Auryn!" I called.

"I've got to go back to the zoo. Poppy was working late, and she thinks she might have seen someone on the CCTV walking around the zoo. It could be a break-in attempt. Before I got the call, I texted around to ask if anyone knows where the Marsdens are," he shouted back up the stairs. I heard his phone beep the next second. "A-ha! Scarlett gave her key to Will. He was supposed to be leaving it here with me after he was done. Apparently there was some family photo album or some such at the house and they wanted to go and get it. Judging by the punctuation of the text, she's pretty surprised they're not back yet. Now, I've really got to go. I promise I'll let you know if anything happens at the zoo." He paused for a second. "Don't go over to that house on your own."

"I'll find someone to go with me, or I won't go at all," I reassured him. "I'll also let you know if the Marsdens return carrying a bloodstained knife to add to their luggage." It was supposed to be a joke, but it came off a little morbid.

"Stay safe," Auryn called before I heard the front door close.

For some reason, the number I dialled first was Katya's. Considering the recent radio silence, I was surprised when she picked up on the second ring.

"What's up? Is everything okay?" she asked, not bothering with the usual preamble.

"It's nothing much, in fact, you're probably too far away," I blustered, losing resolve in the face of her brisk manner.

"I'm fairly close actually. Nothing official, don't worry." She meant she wasn't currently being paid to watch me. "Just driving back from Brighton. I was on a break when you called. What's up?"

I told her as briefly as I could about Timmy's murder and the new information that needed verification before going to the police. I realised that one of the reasons I'd called Katya was because she'd certainly put me straight if she thought I should take what I knew straight to the police, without conducting my own interrogation.

"Sounds sensible. If the police bring her in, she'll clam up. Also, they're less inclined to be economical with the truth as it's unethical," she said, referring to Georgina's planned ruse with the CCTV. "You're looking for backup?"

"How close are you?" I asked and then wondered if I should feel bad about using Katya.

"Ten minutes away from your house. Where's the place?"

I explained and we arranged to meet there.

Fifteen minutes later, I pulled up with Katya's dark Mercedes arriving behind me. I'd told her to park at the entrance to the lane, so that we'd know if there was any funny business going on long before we got to the house.

"Lights are on," she remarked as we approached from the road.

"That's their car." I nodded to the white BMW parked on the drive. "They must still be here. Perhaps the family photo album was harder to locate than expected," I added, but I wasn't convinced.

Katya's hand strayed to her side and I suspected she had a gun concealed there. I knew that things would have to be dire indeed for her to actually use it, as she wasn't officially supposed to be here - and certainly not with me. But I appreciated her having it all the same. As well as being a good moral compass in terms of what to report to the authorities, Katya also counted as my muscle. *I'll really have to work at doing my part for the friendship!* I thought, making a mental note.

Katya stepped forwards, pausing to listen for a moment, before she pressed down on the door handle. She mouthed 'open'. I stood next to her and she pushed open the door.

At first, I couldn't see anyone. The lights inside were blazing and I could certainly see signs that someone had been - and probably still was - inside the house. All of the drawers of the hall table had been wrenched out and their contents was scattered across the hall. The destruction I'd seen in the bedroom was nothing compared to what had gone on here and seemed to be a house-wide occurrence.

I heard something fall down in the kitchen and walked forwards, avoiding treading on any of the scattered debris in the hopes that I wouldn't be heard. Katya moved just as silently behind me, following my steps. The corridor opened up into the kitchen, and I was treated to the curious sight of Will Marsden surrounded by spilled breakfast cereal and dog food, running a hand along the back of the cupboard. He was clearly feeling for something.

I cleared my throat. The guilt on his face when he jumped and turned to see Katya and me would have been amusing, had I not suspected dark motives for his search - and perhaps even motive enough for murder.

"What are you doing here?" Will barked, having the cheek to make it sound as though I was the one in the wrong.

"Scarlett wanted someone to check up on you. Clearly, she had good reason to," I said, looking around at the mess. "Is the family photo album really going to be stashed at the back of the breakfast cereal cupboard?" I let disbelief shine through my voice. To my left, I saw Katya smirk.

"Who the heck is she?" Will growled, nodding at my tall and tough friend.

"My bodyguard. I'm famous you know," I said, just to be obnoxious. Katya's smirk grew and I sensed I'd be in trouble for that remark later.

"More like your accomplice. You came here to burgle my family!"

My mouth dropped open. I shut it again. "First off, you're the one who looks like a burglar right now. And secondly, I have permission to be here to look for you!" Technically, Auryn had permission, but now wasn't the time to be pedantic.

"What's going on?" We all turned to see Lizzie Marsden walk into the kitchen. She was holding an ornate vase I recognised from the landing windowsill.

"These two seem to be accusing us of something, although I have no idea what it is," Will told her.

"Perhaps you can explain why you've decided to trash the house?" I suggested to the newcomer.

"We just wanted some family things," Lizzie claimed. She

looked down at the vase for a moment and then set it on the side. "They're very important to us."

So, she was sticking to her guns.

"That much is obvious," I muttered under my breath. "I actually came here to ask you a question, Lizzie." I had a strong feeling that Lizzie wasn't in her most tell-all mood, but I sincerely doubted I'd get another chance. "We know you were at Oliver's Cafe just around the corner from here on the morning of the murder. There's CCTV footage."

"That's utter nonsense!" Will said, his face darkening to a shade of puce. "Lizzie was at work all day."

I turned to see if his wife had anything to add to the convenient alibi.

"It's like he said," she echoed.

"The camera says otherwise," I told her, hoping I sounded convincing.

"Then go to the police with it," Will sneered. "I doubt they'll be too pleased that you're wasting their time. Come on Lizzie, we're clearly not welcome here - in the home of our family!"

He walked over to the backdoor and wrenched it open before shouting out into the darkness. There was a cacophony of barking and Heinrich appeared running out of the night like a grey ghost. Will shut the door behind the dog and rather pointedly locked it.

"We'll be leaving right away. Is there someone at the house? We wouldn't want to be accused of breaking and entering again," Will said, drenching his voice in sarcasm.

"I'll tell Auryn you're coming." The zoo emergency had to be over by now. He'd be able to get back before the angry couple.

"Well!" Will said, marching past Katya and me without so much as a sideways glance.

"Keys," I said, just as Will was about to walk straight out of the door.

He turned and reached into his pocket before flinging them towards me. Katya reached out and caught them with half a thought before they hit my face. Perhaps she really should consider a career in protection.

As soon as they were out of the door, I called Auryn to warn him that they were on their way back and wouldn't exactly be happy to see him. I told him what I'd caught them doing and suggested he inform Scarlett that the house had been turned upside down in the hunt for... something. I'd looked around when I'd said that and remembered Will feeling along the back of the cupboard. I was again struck by how it must be something small that people seemed to be searching for, but what could it be, and had they found it? Jewellery? Money? Documents? I had no idea what Timmy Marsden might have wanted to hide, but I'd learned better than to make assumptions about people over the past few days.

"Who did you go with?" Auryn asked. The edge in his voice warned me there'd be consequences if I said I'd gone alone - especially considering what I'd found.

"I went with Katya - the police officer from Mallorca, remember? She's back locally but not working."

Katya looked up when she heard her name and then rolled her eyes. We'd had words before about how much I had and hadn't told Auryn about her occupation and the work we'd done together.

"I see. Glad you have someone capable with you," my fiancé said, sounding careful. He knew the score from everything I'd told him before I'd officially been told (I'd been made to sign the Official Secrets Act) and then by inferring everything that came after. We said goodbye and then hung up.

"Do you think they found anything?" I asked Katya. She was peering into the empty cupboard.

"Nope. You saw their faces. They were angry they were interrupted, and from what you've said, they'd have been finished and gone long before now, if they'd found what they were looking for. People only resort to trashing the place if they're getting desperate. Whatever it is, it means a lot to them."

"At least they handed over the key."

"Hmmm," was all Katya had to say to that. I didn't have to be in MI5 to know that she thought it possible that the Marsdens wouldn't have given up their quest at all.

"I'll tell Auryn to warn Scarlett about the possibility of a future break-in." It had got me wondering about the last person to be searching the house. There'd been no signs of a break-in then and I couldn't help but wonder whether Timmy's then-current mistress had been given a key of her own?

Katya turned away from the cupboard with a shrug. "It's easiest to search when you know the people well, although, there are some classic hiding places we can check. People always believe they're being original, but humans mostly think alike." She looked at me hopefully.

I was about to answer when something scratched against the glass door. Both Katya and I jumped around - much to the agent's embarrassment I had no doubt.

"Rameses!" I exclaimed, seeing the pointed ears and Anubis head of the tan hound peering through the window. I opened the door and let the dog in, bending to observe his health. He'd definitely lost weight over the past few days he'd been missing, but due to his normal exercise mostly being limited to running around the garden, he'd definitely been able to afford the loss. Aside from that, there were only a couple of cuts, that looked to have been inflicted by brambles. I checked them and they were healing up fine on their own. Rameses was in remarkably good shape for a dog who'd been on the run in the woods with no experience of surviving in the wild.

Once released, he made a beeline to the dried dog food that littered the floor of the kitchen, courtesy of Will Marsden. I hunted for a lead and then found one hanging by the glass doors. Whilst Rameses was distracted, I hooked it onto his collar. Now that the lost dog had returned, I was taking no chances of his escaping again. I doubted he'd be as fortunate the second time.

"Some good news at last," I told Katya once I'd explained the presence of the dog who'd popped up outside of the door.

"How do you think he got back in?" she asked.

"I assume the same way he got out. Although…" I thought about it some more. "The side gate is definitely closed. I suppose he must have heard Heinrich in the garden - a dog he surely knew - and then jumped back over the fence to say hello.

"I wish my cases were as easy to close," she said with a thin smile. I knew better than to ask beyond that, but it was a sure sign that things weren't going swimmingly for the Secret Service right now.

"Thanks for all of your help," I told my secret agent friend when we were outside the house, and I'd made sure that all doors and windows had been tightly shut. I definitely wouldn't put it past the Marsdens to double back on their way home to Leeds.

"No problem. It's nice to do something that's not work," she said and then blushed, probably realising that catching a crooked couple ransacking a house wasn't exactly a normal way to pass the time.

"Auryn and I are tackling the garden at the house soon. When it's done, you're welcome to come over. We could have a barbecue, or something. I promise we'll talk about anything but work," I reassured her with a twinkle in my eye.

"That sounds nice," Katya confessed and I suddenly got the sense of loneliness from her. I thought I understood why. The company meant keeping quiet about your real work and when it came down to it, what people did for work made up a lot of the conversation. I was sure that Katya found it hard to have friends outside of her job, and I certainly didn't blame her for not having friends within the service. I'd met several of her colleagues and they'd all left a bad taste in my mouth.

"I'll call you when I'm next free?" Katya suggested, and I nodded.

"I'll call you the next time I need a bodyguard," I joked back.

"Next time, you're paying," she replied.

When I arrived back at the house, I was in a remarkably cheerful mood. I hadn't realised how much I'd missed Katya's company. Even though I was friendly to everyone who worked at my zoo and at Avery, I actually didn't have many people I would call genuine friends. Tiff and Auryn were my closest friends but Katya and I had definitely bonded through shared near-death experience and crime solving. In spite of everything, I trusted her, and I wanted her in my life. I hoped she meant what she'd said about calling me when she was available.

The other reason I was feeling perky was due to the presence of Rameses in the backseat of my car. I pulled up outside of Auryn's family home and noted that the Marsdens' car was gone.

"Come on," I said, letting Rameses out. He followed me

meekly across the gravel. Lucky ran out from the side of the house. His tail perked up in the air when he saw us, and he strutted forwards, apparently not even considering that Rameses might be a threat. The dog whined by my side when Lucky approached, but unlike Heinrich, he didn't lunge forwards but stood his ground. Lucky bumped noses with the dog and then flicked his tail in the Pharaoh Hound's face.

"Honestly Lucky, you don't have to rub it in that you're the boss dog," I told my plucky cat. He meowed in response and then trotted off towards the front door. Rameses got up and gently walked after him. Apparently, he'd been accepted as a member of the pack.

Auryn opened the door before I got there. "What on earth happened at Timmy's place? The Marsdens marched in and out without so much as a hello or goodbye. Oh my gosh! You found him!" Auryn had spotted Rameses loitering behind me.

"He scratched at the glass door just after the Marsdens left," I explained. "Their dog had been out in the garden, Perhaps it encouraged him home."

"Thank goodness he's back! I'd better call Scarlett right away."

"As for the Marsdens… I already told you what they were up to. After they left, Katya deduced that they hadn't found what they were looking for."

"Well! I doubt we'll be getting a Christmas card from them after all that."

"I need to call the police," I said, realising that, although I hadn't got a straight answer, the snooping around had definitely added to my suspicions that there was more going on in the Marsden family than I'd ever imagined. Had Lizzie been local on the day that Timmy had died? It could be the final piece of the puzzle.

I dialled the number of the station and then passed along everything I knew to Detective Gregory, who made a point of thanking me for telling him immediately and surprisingly agreed that while a receipt and a vague witness was hardly evidence, conjecture paired with the house search was definitely encouraging him to consider the possibility of the pair whom no one had suspected.

"Scarlett asked if we can keep the dog. Apparently because we 'have zoos, right?' it will be no trouble at all." Auryn raised an eyebrow.

I looked down at the Pharaoh Hound, who was starting to eye Lucky with a lot more interest now that the cat had his back turned. Something told me we might be playing a dangerous game.

"I suppose we shouldn't have expected anything else." Scarlett had perfected the art of delegation. She had Georgina running around trying to get her off the hook as a murder suspect, and now she was using us to care for a dog that by rights should be her problem. I was willing to bet that it was this skill that had made her underwear company such a success. She oversaw everything without actually doing any of the actual grunt work.

She never got her hands dirty... and that was why I found it very hard to believe that Scarlett Marsden had killed her husband.

8

ARTS AND CRAFTS

I woke up to loud barking on the day of the arts and crafts event. I opened an eye in time to see Lucky arrive in the bedroom and jump up on the bed in a surprisingly sedate manner. He was followed by Rameses, who was still making a racket. Three red lines across his nose hinted at what had befallen him.

"I hope one of you learned a lesson," I said, being sure to note that beyond loud complaining and a scratch I needed to clean, no one seemed too hurt. However, I didn't think my stress levels would benefit from it being a permanent thing. Both Lucky and Rameses were grown up animals who were used to their own space. Auryn shot me a look that said much the same. Scarlett was going to have to take a little more responsibility at some point.

"I'll take Lucky to The Lucky Zoo as planned. You'd better bring Rameses to Avery Zoo." I bit my lip. Dogs were very definitely not usually permitted at the zoo, and I knew no one was going to think Rameses was a service dog in a million years. "You'd better say he's a new character in the comic - a nemesis for Lucky to fight against. It's not too far from the truth. I'll have to add it in."

Auryn gave me the thumbs up and then muttered something about getting going early in order to buy some dog food for Rameses. I hadn't thought to take any home after his meal last night - especially as I hadn't known he was going to be staying with us.

"Auryn..." My fiancé turned back in the bedroom doorway to look at me with bleary eyes. "It's going to be a great day," I told him with conviction I was determined to carry through the event. It was going to go well.

It had to go well, or my zoo was going to find itself in a lot of trouble. There was only so much piggybacking off Avery's success that we could do. I hoped today would be the day we stood out as a place to come back and visit, and hey - maybe tell your friends about, too. It was sink or swim for The Lucky Zoo.

As soon as I saw the sunshine and looked at the weather forecast for the day ahead I marked it as a mini success. No matter how much promotion and ticket selling you did, nothing was worse than torrential rain on a day that required zoo animals be visible and paper, preferably, stayed dry.

I'd never considered myself to be a skulker, but today I was going to make a special effort to be visible and move around the zoo, just chatting to people. I'd watched Auryn do it many times before, but although I'd expected it to be a challenge, I hadn't bargained for the near-constant mob who seemed determined to follow me anywhere and everywhere, all trying to shout questions at me, or ask if I could get their manuscript published (probably not).

I was always pleased that my comic brought happiness to people, and that my fame could be used to encourage visitors to the zoo, who in turn learned about animal conservation, but these people were different. The artists I wanted to talk to, who were dotted around the zoo getting on with their entries, shot me apologetic smiles when I walked past. In the end, I turned around and flatly asked my hangers on how many of them had started on their art or craft projects for the day. A few of them muttered something about not being here for that nonsense. For just a second, I saw a flash of red behind my eyes. Then I took a deep breath. Today I was on show. I could be nothing but professional.

"I am here to give feedback to people who are creating art and would like to hear it. I'm also walking around to check progress and make sure everything is going okay. Please remember I am the owner of this zoo as well as a comic book writer." I managed a tight smile. "Aside from that, you are of course welcome to come and watch the talk I'll be giving later this morning here and early in the afternoon at Avery Zoo. I'm sure many of your questions will be answered during the talk, and there'll be plenty of time afterwards for me to answer any that might have been missed."

I looked around at the group, rather pleased by the tactful way I'd brushed them off. Unfortunately, they didn't appear to be moving.

"Madigan! Is that you in there?" a cheery woman called. Gloria Lenin had a shining black pixie cut and a body large enough to bump most of my hangers-on out of the way. "Wonderful to see you, dear," she said, reaching out and enveloping me in her large mass. Gloria was my main point of contact at LightStrike Publishing House. Fortunately, she was also my favourite company member. I'd grown to loathe the self-righteous woman who answered the phones and seemed to view herself as some kind of gatekeeper who kept troublesome authors safely at bay. I'd been close to throwing in the towel with my publishers all together when she'd made it sound like I was making a huge fuss over nothing with regard to the ridiculous publicist I'd been assigned.

"Hi Madi," Gloria's smaller assistant Gareth said, shooting me a little smile whilst trying to maintain the balance of several files and pieces of cardboard he'd been tasked with carrying.

"Wonderful day, wonderful people," Gloria said, shining at everyone in turn. "You must show me the venue for our little publishing talk. I think it's going to be jolly good fun!" Everything was always 'jolly good fun' when it came to Gloria. It was morbid, but there was definitely a part of me that wanted to see what would happen if she ever had to attend a funeral, or worse - give a speech at one!

"You're a publisher?" one of the watchers said.

"You're her publisher?" another piped up.

"I am a representative from the company in charge of printing and publishing *Monday's Menagerie*." She held up a hand to quell the clamour. "However, I am not an agent, and neither is Madi. Her success story is exceptional, which is something I am going to be making very clear in my talk later on today. If you want to be published, don't hang around industry people without bothering to do a speck of research." She shook her head, still smiling. "Do your home-work and keep working at it. That's how success stories happen!"

"She got famous overnight," I heard someone mutter.

"If you come to my talk, you'll find out that I wrote the comic for years online. And I still do publish online."

"What? For free?" another follower asked. "Isn't that devaluing your work?"

Honestly, I wanted nothing more than to tell her to put a sock in it - especially in front of my publisher!

Instead I took another deep breath. "There's a fine line between give and take. The content on the website is different from the published books. A lot of people like both, but some choose just the website and others just the printed book."

"Soon to be books!" Gloria piped up, making me want to put a sock in her mouth, too.

"Giving away freebies can help to build your audience. I initially wasn't treating it as a business. I was lucky enough to have friends who helped me to start monetising by selling prints and original sketches from the comics to super fans, and then I was fortunate enough to be spotted by an agent. I'll be the first to admit that there was a bit of luck involved in my success..." a whole lot of secrets and lies, too, but I couldn't share the truth, "... but there was also a lot of hard work that went into building the foundation of the comic. The first ever volume that got published was done using a crowd-funding campaign."

"Man, I bet those books are worth big money now," one of the followers said. I ignored her.

"You'll hear all about it if you come to the talk. If I say any more, you'll be bored!" I smiled weakly.

"You heard the lady! Scoot! I want to see those pencils on some paper," Gloria said, managing to sound cheery, even as she essentially sent the group packing.

When the crowd was clear she turned to me and raised her eyebrows. "I don't hold out much hope for their careers! Hanging off your coattails is not the way to success."

I sighed. "There are a lot of desperate people out there in the creative world. It's tough. You can be great at creating things but not have a single clue about how to run a business. Some people can't do both." I hesitated. "I wouldn't say it's a strength of mine. I've just hired a marketing guy to deal with all of that for the zoo.

Gloria looked surprised. "Just the one?"

"Well… I've still got a lot of hiring to do, but I'm doing it gradually. The first focus is the animals and, well…"

"You can afford to run at a loss for a while," Gloria observed. "It all looks fabulous anyway! There are so many people here. I think I might actually be getting a little stage-fright," she joked.

I smiled in return. Gloria Lenin had probably shaken the hand of everyone in the delivery room when she'd been born. I was surprised that the word 'stage-fright' was even in her vocabulary.

I took her through the zoo and then showed her the venue - which was simply the largest patch of eco-mat covered space in the zoo. As publishing houses went Light-Strike were still relatively small players, although not so small that Gloria didn't look very taken aback by my choice of venue.

"It's so… open!" was the best positive comment she was able to lay her hands on.

"There's going to be a little stage set up when it's time for the talks. And there's a PA system, too. I'm not sure we've thought about whether or not any slides will be visible on the projector though… but I had an idea that we'd email them to all attendees, so they can look at them on their phones," I finished brightly.

"Well… jolly good!" she said, using her catchphrase. "Now, how's the new book coming on?"

From then on, it was down to business until the morning rolled along and I took to the stage for my talk about *Monday's Menagerie's* rise to success.

As soon as that was over, I handed the microphone to Gloria and Gareth and then rushed off to give the same talk at Avery Zoo for the other half of the attendees. I was pleased to see that Avery Zoo was busy, but not any more so than

The Lucky Zoo. A deep rooted worry I hadn't even known I'd been holding onto seemed to lift from my shoulders.

It was only after my talk finished and I thought about the packed outside area and the packed play barn that I realised just how many people I'd addressed today. I was well-versed in press conferences by now, and the company had signed me up for a couple of comic convention panels later in the summer, but I'd never expected to get such a large and positive reaction on my home turf, so to speak. It made me realise how far I'd come.

Gloria was doing her best to drive it home, too, by telling me that while my new comics were good, I really needed to knuckle down and finish the thing. After the uplifting observation I'd made today, I thought I might actually make time to do just that.

Tiff found me after the talk when I was on my way back to the car park. There was a lot of running around involved in this joint zoo event! Then there'd be the judging, which was thankfully taking place at The Lucky Zoo, due to its larger surface area and 'stage'. The benefits of not having a proper venue with walls was that there were no walls! People could pack in anyway they wanted.

"Madi!" she called right before I was about to walk into the reception area.

"Hi, it's going well, isn't it? How was your talk?" Tiff had been on right before me and I'd been sorry to miss it due to my own Q and A session overrunning.

"It was great! Everyone was really excited about my Etsy sales and what I did to make it all happen."

"That's great! It's been going well then?" I asked realising I hadn't talked to Tiff about our creative side projects, as we'd liked to call them, for quite some time. It wasn't because I didn't care about Tiff's work, I just didn't want to turn into someone who went on and on about her own achievements whilst unknowingly belittling the achievements of those around me.

"Yeah, everything's been brilliant. Great for the savings account! Look at us, both millennials bucking the trend and actually having two coins to rub together," she joked.

"Urgh!" was all I had to say in response to that. It always irked me to have my fate thrown in with that of an entire generation. Even so, I retained hope that one day the millennials would rise up and achieve more than anyone ever imagined they could - and all whilst propping up the avocado and toast industry.

"Have you been on anymore dates with Detective Gregory? He seemed really nice," I said, remembering that I owed him. More than that, I felt he probably deserved to have a good word put in. I'd been unsure about Alex Gregory when we'd first met, but his recent actions had reassured me.

"We've got a proper date scheduled for tonight. I told him about the arts and crafts day and the talk I was giving." She blushed a little. "He was really impressed and said he wanted to come. Only... the murder case."

"At least you're going out tonight. You'll be able to tell him how awesome you are."

"I think he already knows how awesome I am," she said, surprising me with the wry smile that lit up her face. No wonder Detective Gregory had been so keen to see her again! Their last date must have gone very well indeed.

"What about Pierce?" I asked, wondering if he'd ever completed his 'follow up'.

Pierce was still very much a mystery. Since employing him, he'd popped in and out of the zoo, but was always quiet about exactly what he was working on. I might have accused him of wasting my time had I not set him up with a unique promotion code for tickets for today's event and asked him if he could do anything with it. I'd known it was short notice and had been prepared to give him a code he could promote for the next zoo event in the calendar, but he'd just shrugged and said it was no problem. When he'd managed to sell an extra hundred tickets for The Lucky Zoo's side of the event I'd been very impressed - but I still remained mystified.

"I went out with him for a drink last night," Tiff revealed. "It was nice. Pierce is a great guy, don't get me wrong." I knew she was mincing words because he was my employee.

"What is it?" I asked, preferring that she just tell me straight.

"He's almost too perfect. It's ridiculous, I know, but he makes me feel inadequate. Everything about him is slick and polished. We've been out twice, and both times he's chatted to a waiter or the man behind the bar, and by the end of the night you'd think they were best friends. It gets him all kinds of special treatment, which is nice, but it's... it's sort of hard to keep up with in a way."

I nodded understandingly. "You won't believe the number of tickets he managed to sell in under a week for The Lucky Zoo's arts and crafts side of things. In the end, I think it pushed us to outsell Avery."

"Auryn will be jealous," Tiff said with a grin.

"No doubt, although, it might help him with our wager." I shook my head. "This is probably going to sound equally ridiculous, but it's almost too good to be true, you know?"

"Do you think he's involved with *them*?" Tiff said, probably implying the government.

I shrugged and pulled a face. "These days, I keep an open mind about everything, but I don't see why helping me to sell tickets would benefit *them*. Who knows? Perhaps we really are being silly. But the detective is nice, isn't he?"

"You keep saying that. What the heck has he done to you?"

Oh, the joys of having a perceptive friend. "It's more what he hasn't done," I said and briefly explained my flouting of civil duty.

"He really does sound like a nice man. That or he likes me even more than I thought," she added with an unselfconscious grin.

"I know which one I'm betting on," I joked.

"So, that's why you're so keen to push me towards him. You want law enforcement on your side! I am shocked and outraged." Tiff pretended to be shocked and outraged. She looked moderately constipated, but in a charming way (how was that possible?!). "To be fair... you do have a knack for getting into trouble."

"Don't I just know it," I replied, but I reflected that for once, everything had gone to plan. The judging was nearly upon us and, if luck held, the day would end with no escaped animals, no major medical emergencies, and a financial success story for both zoos.

When the last few visitors were leaving The Lucky Zoo and all of the awards had been given out, Auryn and I took a trip around the elephant enclosure.

"I swear this is such a brilliant enclosure design. You outdid yourself. Elephants are such beautiful but large animals. I don't know why, but you always forget that when you see them stuffed into zoos who don't have enough space to accommodate them properly. Here it's different. You can still see them really well because of the way the area is designed, but it's more like watching a group of wild animals.

They're not used to you and you just hope that they'll trust you enough to come a little closer. It's not a certainty but a treat when it happens. That's the way zoos should be, I think."

"You do all right at Avery," I reassured him. Yes, it was lovely that the elephants, big cats, and other larger animals at The Lucky Zoo had space enough to roam a lot further than many of their captive comrades, but not all animals needed endless space and many actively did well when human interaction was involved. The crux of the matter was, you always had to compromise. No matter how hard you tried, a zoo was a zoo and the wild was the wild. All you could strive to do was find a happy medium.

"It was a great day," I reminded him when the mood started to feel sombre.

Auryn and I watched the swallows swooping low to catch insects, and I tilted my head back to examine the sky. I didn't feel the pressure build up before the storm, the way I usually did, but the low-flying birds after their sluggish prey suggested that something was on its way. I liked to think that the torrential rain in-between the sun made you appreciate those lazy summer days that bit more, but perhaps that was just my British optimism. If I had a penny for every time I'd heard someone say 'it's just a shower' whilst monsoon level rain drenched summer events, I'd probably have a fortune close in size to the one that was sitting in my bank account right now.

"This is just the start. Everything's going to go right for us," Auryn said, echoing my line of thought. "Well... almost everything."

"Almost everything?" I repeated.

"Everything is going to go right... except for your restaurant. That's going to do terribly," he teased.

"You just wait and see," I batted back with a smile. I had

145

big plans, and with a mysterious marketing genius on my side, I also had the winning edge.

And all I'd have to do was ask him to take a break from making The Lucky Zoo too darn successful and focus his efforts on the restaurant instead.

Auryn was going to be blown out of the water.

9

OH DEER!

The house phone rang the next morning while Auryn was in the shower. I answered it to find that it was Jon Walker-Reed. After I'd explained why Auryn hadn't answered his mobile, I told him about the state the house had been left in after Will and Lizzie had left. To my knowledge, neither of them had been arrested yet, but I was hopeful that the police were doing everything they could to find evidence that would place either, or both of them, in the area at the time of Timmy's death. Or perhaps the man in the cafe would turn out to be wrong. It was a police matter now, and I was rather glad to be rid of the couple.

"Heavens! I heard it on the grapevine that Will wanted something or other at the house and then robbed the place. Believe me, it's quite the scandal at the moment. I didn't realise they'd trashed it, too."

"I don't think anything was actually taken," I said, bemused by the way gossip morphed the truth into something completely else.

"That's awful. I was never that friendly with Will at school," Jon said, conveniently distancing himself from the dead man's brother. If this was the reaction to a moderate offence, I wouldn't like to be the person who'd committed murder. They were going to find they were friendless as well as fettered. "At least he was never invited into The Lords of the Downs. Will separated himself from Timmy's parents as soon as he was free of education. He still got an inheritance, but his attitude made him an unsuitable choice - not to mention that he also moved to the back end of nowhere." Jon paused for thought. "We should really do something for Scarlett. Perhaps we could club together and pay for a cleaner to sort out the mess? I almost feel like we're the ones responsible. If only I'd gone round to pick him up and dragged him to the club in spite of his excuses..."

"...you might have ended up just as dead as Timmy," I finished, knowing that regret was a dark path to walk down.

"Yes... perhaps you're right," Jon admitted. "But we really should do something. I know Scarlett. If she hasn't been back to the house by now it means she's not going back at all. She'll let it stay how it is and sell it as seen. While cleaning the place would do someone's bank balance a favour, it might do even better for Timmy's memory - if you know what I'm saying."

I believed I did know what he was saying. I suspected at least two separate unsolicited searches of the house had been carried out after the murder. It was possible that neither searcher had found what they were looking for, but that didn't mean it would hold true for future hunters. "It would do *someone's* bank balance a favour?" I clarified, having picked up on the way Jon hadn't specified that the proceeds from the sale of the house would go to Scarlett Marsden.

Jon cleared his throat awkwardly. I realised he hadn't meant to let it slip. "I'm not sure of anything. All I know is that when we were at the barbecue after Timmy drank that bowl of punch, he said something about cutting out people who didn't really love him and making sure that when his time came, the money would go to someone who actually deserved it."

My heart dropped what felt like a mile. "How loudly did he say it?"

"Quite loudly," Jon said, sounding solemn.

"Did you tell the police?"

"I didn't think it was relevant. Honestly, I thought it was just talk until now. Timmy was a rather dramatic drunk. But with all of this business about the house being turned upside down... I don't know what to think."

"Auryn and I will do it. Auryn knew Timmy pretty well, and you know you can trust us, right?" When Jon hesitated, I continued. "You were with us at the time of Timmy's murder."

"Of course... I wasn't doubting you for a second. It just sounds like a lot of work. Shouldn't we pay someone?"

"Do you really think it's a good idea to bring someone else into the mix when we have no idea what could be in the house?" I hoped it was a rhetorical question.

"I suppose you have a point. I'll suggest it to Scarlett."

There was a knock at the door and I told Jon to hang on whilst I answered it.

I opened the door and then lifted the phone back to my ear. "No need to ask Scarlett. She's just arrived, so I'll suggest it myself," I said, smiling at the woman on the doorstep. She looked a lot more impressive than the day I'd encountered her coming out of her lover's house. She was also more formally attired than she had been at the barbecue, where Timmy had allegedly spoken so loudly and harshly about how he was going to pass on his legacy.

"Hi," Scarlett said, smiling at me. It looked a little wobbly. That's when it sort of hit me for the first time that Scarlett, for all of her and Timmy's faults, had lost her husband. "I just wanted to check on Rameses. I promise I'm doing everything I can to arrange for him to come and live with me. I just need a few more days. Thank you for keeping him for me."

"It's our pleasure," I said, politely not mentioning the trouble there'd been between Lucky and the dog. Hopefully Scarlett wouldn't notice or comment on the scratches on the dog's nose. "You wouldn't happen to know if Rameses had ever escaped before, would you? It will be something to bear in mind when you make arrangements for him."

"If he ever got out before, I never heard anything about it."

The Pharaoh Hound materialised in the hallway and cocked his head when he saw Scarlett. The next moment he was running towards her with his whip-like tail wagging from side to side.

"He was always Timmy's dog. I hope he'll get used to being mine," she said.

"I think he's already showing who he's meant to be with," I reassured her.

Scarlett ruffled Rameses' large, pointed ears and focused on the dog. "I did love him, you know," she said. It took me a couple of seconds to realise she was talking about Timmy. "I know what everyone thinks, but we loved each other. We had something that worked for us and I'm just devastated that he's gone." She gave the dog one final pat before pulling herself back upright. "Now Rameses is all I've got left."

"Have the police got any ideas as to who might have done it?" I asked as carefully as I could. I'd already decided that Scarlett was innocent - well, innocent of murder at least.

"No. It feels like they aren't doing anything! I can't believe it."

"Who do you think killed him?" I knew it was probably insensitive, but if Scarlett had some idea, it could help put a few things together. And after the third degree she'd been given by the police, I wouldn't have been surprised if she'd kept it to herself.

"I wish I did! They wouldn't be walking around free if that were the case. Everyone loved Timmy, apart from those that didn't, if you know what I mean." She arched a perfect eyebrow. "He rubbed people up the wrong way sometimes, but I can't recall anything that might inspire what someone did to him. Although you wouldn't know it the way his family are behaving!"

"About that… Auryn and I would like to offer to tidy things up at the house. Jon said you might be selling?"

Scarlett nodded. "It's likely. It was always Timmy's house, not mine." Her lips thinned for a moment, and I wondered if she knew about what may or may not have been written in Timmy's will, or if she even cared. It didn't strike me that a businesswoman as successful as Scarlett would be particularly cut up over what her husband did and didn't bequeath to her. But was the business still as successful as appearances suggested?

I remembered the contract Jon had mentioned. It had been a company merger. I'd assumed that her company was taking over another one, but what if I'd made the wrong assumption? Had that ever been mentioned explicitly? If Scarlett's company had taken the hit, it could make Timmy's will a more important factor. I shut the lid on that theory. I still didn't believe Scarlett would have got her hands dirty. Not with her manicure! *But it wouldn't be completely out of character for her to have employed someone else to do the job for her,* I suddenly realised.

Scarlett had been talking whilst I'd been musing about murder.

"Sorry, would you mind saying that again?" I asked.

"I was saying, don't put yourself out cleaning up. It's very sweet of you to offer, but I know you're both busy people."

"It's no problem at all. Auryn and I had planned to take a few days off to do some tidying up of our own. Anyway, we need to swing by to pick up some more dog food for Rameses." I knew for a fact that the dog food was currently strewn all over the kitchen floor, but I was banking on Scarlett not having visited the house.

"Well, if you're sure. You've still got the key, haven't you? I was actually coming by to get it, but you can keep it for a while. I'll pick it up when I've sorted things out for me and Rameses." She smiled down at the hound, who looked lovingly up at her.

I half-wished that Lucky was present to meet Scarlett. Dogs could be fond of all kinds of horrible people, but cats had a knack for looking at a person and knowing whether they could or couldn't be trusted.

"Thank you so much!" Scarlett waved a hand and then walked out of the house back to her sports car.

Rameses whined a little when she started up the engine and drove away.

"Don't worry, everything will be all right in the end," I said, hoping it would be true for both of us.

"What exactly did you tell Scarlett we were doing?" Auryn asked when we arrived at the house later that day. I'd told him we were taking the day off, and he'd agreed it was probably as good a time as any. Our big event had been a success, and what was the point of being business owners if we couldn't take time off when we wanted to? Normal people got weekends... we got a handful of days scattered through the year. At least - that was the way it looked so far. It was like an exhibition of workaholics.

"I said we'd tidy up so that things look neat for her selling the house."

He pushed open the door and we looked in at the general disarray. "Tidy things up? It looks more like an industrial cleaning job."

"It'll be fine once we get going," I told him breezily. "Oh, if there's any surviving dog food, we should grab it, but I think it was all spilled. Will Marsden must have thought Timmy had hidden something in there." I shook my head. He'd clearly been desperate. "We should get his food and water bowl, too." Rameses had been dropped off at Avery Zoo on the way over. Tiff had offered to babysit.

Auryn's eyes had sharpened when I'd mentioned Will Marsden looking through the dog food. "That's why we're really here, isn't it?" he said. "You want to find whatever they were looking for."

I turned and leant against the kitchen unit. "Isn't it better that someone like us finds whatever it is? Especially if it's something bad…"

"I should have known you had an ulterior motive. You never want to clean!"

"Hey, I'm not that bad!" I protested, but it was weak. "We'd better get started. Who knows? We might find nothing at all."

But in the end, we found quite a lot.

I was upstairs tidying the bedroom when I came across my first find. Something had been taped to the back of one of the dresser draws. I pulled it out and opened up an old leather wallet, only to discover that its contents held something quite different from its original intended purpose. A stack of polaroids spilled out from the banknotes section. It took me a second or two to realise what I was looking at due to the closeup nature of some of the shots.

"Oh… oh no," I said, pulling a face. In some ways, I was

glad I couldn't recognise some of the women pictured. In other ways, I was horrified. I was about to look through to see if there were any recognisable shots (as it would definitely count as a motive for murder!) when a blast of music echoed through the house.

"Sorry!" Auryn shouted a second later. "I just thought a tune or two might help this to go a bit faster."

I walked downstairs to find that Taylor Swift was playing at a far more comfortable level than before. "I found some photos."

"I gather they weren't very nice?" Auryn said when he saw my expression.

"Not something to go in the family photo album, no." I sighed and shook my head. I'd come downstairs to give myself a moment to recover before I looked at any more of the pictures to see if there were any recognisable subjects. I listened to Taylor singing about how she 'knew this man was trouble but had decided to give him a whirl for the heck of it' for a few seconds before it hit me.

"Did you change the CD when you turned on the sound system?"

"Nope," Auryn said. "That's why I'm not deaf in one ear. Timmy or Scarlett must have liked listening to Tay Tay at full volume." I silently raised an eyebrow at Auryn's use of slang. He was definitely a closet Swifty.

"Huh! And it's just Taylor Swift on the CD?"

Auryn held up a jewel case for the album the song had come from.

I felt my forehead crease as I frowned at the memory of Andy Wright describing his almost-visit to the house on the morning of Timmy's death. He'd claimed he'd heard the dog barking and then some shouting - but maybe it had just been the style of singing on the classic rock songs he'd heard. From that description, I couldn't be sure that it had been classic rock that Andy had heard - but he certainly hadn't been describing Taylor Swift. Had he been lying? I wondered. I couldn't think of a single reason why he would lie about the sort of music that was playing. Otherwise, why mention it at all?

Auryn shot me a questioning look but I shook my head. I thought it was strange, but I had no idea what it meant.

Back upstairs, I continued my inspection of the polaroids and discovered that amongst the close ups there were also some handy full body shots. I sighed when I recognised Annabelle Wright and Officer Kelly Lane. I'd worried that Officer Kelly might be closer to the case than she should be, and now I had my proof.

I put the photos to one side and resolved to tidy the rest of the room whilst I thought about what to do with my discovery. I was examining an exceedingly tacky pair of fluffy handcuffs and a pair of bunny girl ears - that I just couldn't imagine Scarlett wearing - when the decision was taken from me.

"Police! You're trespassing on private property!"

I turned around and saw my own look of surprise and recognition reflected on Officer Kelly Lane's face.

I took a quick step to the side, so that the pile of polaroids I'd placed on the dresser remained hidden for now. "I'm here with Auryn. We've got permission from Scarlett Marsden. I have a key!" I showed her.

Officer Kelly's shoulders relaxed. "Sorry about that. One of the neighbours reported seeing you go into the house. They can't have recognised you."

"I don't suppose they saw anything on the day of the murder?"

"No... it's funny really. They probably never paid their neighbours any mind until now. Nothing like a murder to spark interest in the comings and goings of the people who live near you."

I nodded my agreement, but my mind was elsewhere. I'd locked the front door behind me when we'd gone into the house. It wasn't the sort of thing I was in the habit of doing, but there'd been a voice in my head that whispered if the Marsdens or anyone else came back, at least Auryn would see them coming if they had to walk all the way around the back. The police had announced the house was no longer a crime scene, so they would have surely handed back any keys giving them access. But Officer Kelly had got in.

My uncertainty must have shown on my face.

"I didn't kill him," she said, and then walked over and sat down on the bed. "I thought I loved him. Things actually ended between us a short while ago. That's why I thought I'd be fine to work on the case. I thought it was just a matter of being professional, but I've bungled it, haven't I? Coming in here with a key I'm not supposed to have." She looked down at the floor. I wondered if she was being completely truthful about the status of her and Timmy's fling - her actions hinted that it was far from over - but I could appreciate that she was trying to behave in a responsible manner.

"I'm glad you're here. I need some professional advice…" I said, walking over to the dresser and picking up the stack of photos. "I'm afraid you're in here." I handed them over.

Officer Kelly flicked through them without a word.

"The only other person I recognise is Annabelle Wright, and I happen to know she has an airtight alibi."

I sat down on the bed next to her. "I suppose there's not a lot more you can get from the photos then, unless anyone recognises any of the closeups, but you can't exactly flash them around town. And anyway, if you knew you were in one of the photos but couldn't possibly be recognised, you wouldn't be too fussed, would you? I mean... you wouldn't murder someone over it."

Officer Kelly shrugged. "Timmy Marsden might have threatened to use them as blackmail. Or maybe he sent a more recognisable photo to one of his fling's partners, and the partner was none too happy about it." She frowned. "What about that club he was supposed to be joining?"

"They would not be thrilled to find out about this. The Lords of the Downs is supposed to be made up of respectable and upstanding gentlemen. Although, that's not to say one of them didn't kill him. Maybe someone really didn't want him to join the club."

"That seems a bit excessive."

I shrugged. I thought the whole concept behind the club was fairly ridiculous, but that didn't mean the members felt the same way.

"Why do you think he kept all this?" I asked, hoping for some insight from someone who'd been with Timmy.

"Trophies, I suppose. That's usually the reason. I, er... actually wasn't expecting to find anyone in the house when I came in and heard the music. There never was a tip off," she confessed.

I nodded understandingly. Officer Kelly had been here to search, along with the rest of them. Annabelle Wright may have an airtight alibi for the murder, but if Officer Kelly had a key to the house I was willing to bet that as Timmy's then-current fling, Annabelle would have her own, too. She'd wanted her pictures back.

"So, what should we do about the photos?" I asked.

"I don't think there's anything to be learned from them," the police officer said with a sigh. "Unless you think I had something to do with it, in which case, I would understand if you handed over the photo of me." She was serious when she said it, but her eyes told me just how pained she felt about the idea of her colleagues seeing her at her most vulnerable.

"No, we'll destroy them." I could be making a mistake, but if my gut feeling that she was innocent proved correct and I handed those photos in, it would condemn her to ridicule at the very least, and at the most, it could ruin her career. I wasn't willing to do that to another person, especially when I saw nothing to suggest that they were guilty, beyond some sordid snapshots.

"Thank you," the police officer said, looking relieved. "I'll help you tidy up. Just in case there is something useful in here."

"Didn't the police look up here?" I asked.

"Sure, but there was no reason to believe there was anything hidden, so it wasn't done with a fine tooth comb. We're trained to look at what's in front of us and make an assessment."

"Well, Timmy was pretty good at hiding stuff," I allowed. The wallet had been taped to the back of a drawer and the handcuffs and bunny ears had been concealed inside an interior pocket of an ancient waterproof coat.

"Let's see if there's anything else to find…"

We tidied and we found a few more things. There was another stack of photos behind a different drawer - this time featuring men - and I acknowledged that I'd known less about the Marsdens' relationship than I'd ever realised. Now I knew more than I wanted. There'd also been a couple of items that looked like they'd belonged to women other than Scarlett - including an old gym membership card made out for Shona Pleasant. I'd raised an eyebrow at that one.

After some brief consideration, those photos went in the trash, too. I was left with an image of Detective Treesden I knew would scar my mind forever. It was a good thing he was now retired. I doubted I'd be able to look him in the eye again!

Aside from that, there'd been a photo of a fully-clothed woman, hidden behind the picture framed on the wall of the bedroom. The trouble that had been taken to conceal it made me think it was important, but I had no idea why. All that was written on the back was the name 'Thea Oatway'. That was one photo Officer Kelly and I decided to keep, as it could be something important.

"I haven't found anything that relates to Will and Lizzie Marsden," I said when we'd finished the room. Auryn had popped up from the kitchen to bring me tea and then come back with another cup when he'd realised we had company, but he hadn't shouted that he'd found anything either.

"Perhaps it was the photo of this woman that they were after," Officer Kelly mused.

"It hardly seems worth turning the house upside down for. Not when we can't make head nor tail of it!"

"Maybe they thought Timmy had something but really he didn't. Or maybe someone got there first."

I considered both options but was no closer to working out the truth.

"He was going to help me with my career, you know," Officer Kelly shared right before we walked out of the now-tidy bedroom.

"How?"

"His family is old and well respected in these parts. You know how it is… old money and old school rules, especially in a rural area like the one we live in. He promised me he'd put a word in the right ears when he could." Her smile faded a little. "It's always nice to think you'll be getting a leg up, but I'll achieve the same with hard work. I know I will."

"Of course you will," I reassured her, hoping it was the truth. It was news to me that Timmy Marsden had any kind of contacts or leverage, but perhaps he'd believed it would change once he was a member of The Lords of the Downs. More worryingly, perhaps he was right. My opinion of the men-only club was sinking ever lower.

"Find anything?" Auryn asked when we came downstairs.

I exchanged a look with Officer Kelly.

"Probably nothing that will help the case," she said, tactfully.

Auryn saw the bin liner in my hand but made no comment.

"Nothing down here apart from an ocean of wasted dog food. We should have brought Rameses here with us so it wouldn't all go to waste. We're going to have to pick up some fresh stuff on the way home. On the plus side, I've got the size, shape, and even the taste ingrained in my mind, so there's no way we'll get the wrong stuff." When I raised an eyebrow at him he shook his head. "Don't ask."

We all had another cup of tea. For a time, we drank in silence, each mulling over our separate thoughts. I was reflecting that a man had died, right by the glass doors just a couple of metres away from us, and thus far, no one had been brought to justice for committing that crime.

"Gosh, that's hideous!" Officer Kelly suddenly announced, breaking the silence.

I followed her line of sight to the stag's head, mounted on the wall.

"Did Timmy like to hunt?" I asked Auryn, well aware of the preferred pastimes of many of his old school friends. I was no vegetarian, and I heartily approved of sustainable game hunting, as those animals sure as heck had better lives than chickens kept in crates, but I did abhor killing for the sake of killing, or any form of bloodsport.

"No, that was never Timmy's bag. He used to like riding when we were at school, but he always claimed he was a pacifist. His older brother Will was a bit of a crack-shot. I don't know if he still hunts, but I'd wager that stag was either courtesy of him or their father. I couldn't say which," Auryn said.

"You think it might be from Will?" I stood up and walked up to the mounted head. I hadn't considered it before because it was just something that people who were friends with Auryn seemed to possess. I'd even once jokingly asked him if there was a shop that specialised in selling decapitated animal heads, regardless of whether or not you'd personally killed them. The house where Auryn and I lived had had its fair share of morbid trophies when I'd moved in. They were now all in the attic, where they'd remain forever more. Just because I approved of sustainable hunting didn't mean I approved of showing off grisly remains after the event.

I made to lift the heavy mount off the wall and found Auryn by my side. Any other time, I'd probably have protested that I could do it by myself. I wasn't that small. But something about the stag intrigued me.

"That antler's a bit wobbly," I muttered and gave it a yank. It came clean off, and it was with mixed dread and elation that I realised there was something rolled up inside of the antler.

I pulled it out and unrolled the sheaf of paper.

Last Will and Testament of Timothy Robert Marsden

I lowered the papers for a moment. I had no idea if Timmy had another will somewhere else, but this one was dated a couple of weeks prior to his death. In fact, if memory served, it would have been written and signed the day before the barbecue, where Timmy had allegedly drunkenly boasted that his family's money was going to go to a deserving cause.

I was about to find out what that cause was.

I walked back over to the kitchen counter and unfolded the papers where they could all see. Below the initial heading that I'd already read, a letter had been stapled. I read it and realised that it was a contract of agreement for putting a child up for adoption. The name of the child listed was Sally Marsden. I sucked in a breath when I read the last name. Had Timmy fathered a child no one knew about and then persuaded the mother to give it away? I read down the letter, hoping to see the names of the mother and father listed somewhere.

"Oh... oh no... Timmy, you didn't!" Auryn said, having read the names at the same time as I had. Timmy's name was listed as the father and his signature was below it releasing the child. The name printed next to his was Elizabeth Field.

I looked at Auryn for confirmation.

"I'm not sure," he confessed. "All I know is that Will and Lizzie met because Lizzie was friends with Timmy through riding. Somehow, she met Will through him. Years later, they ended up married. I've no idea what happened in-between. Timmy said he was quitting riding as soon as he went on his gap year, which turned into gap years. After that, he met Scarlett at a party, funded her startup idea, and the rest is history. At least - that last part is the story he shared with me when we reconnected after all these years."

"Do you really think it might be possible that Elizabeth Field and Lizzie Marsden could be one and the same?" I asked.

Auryn screwed up his face. "When we were still studying, Timmy used to boast about all of the girls he met through his fancy riding events that he went to - especially women older than we were. I thought he was just saying it to impress us, but it looks like there was some truth to it." He pointed to the date on the adoption form. "Timmy would have been in sixth form."

"Too young to look after a baby," I acknowledged. It was clear that the mother had hardly been ready for it either.

"There are a lot of years I can't account for," Auryn said. He'd been out of contact with his friends for a long time, and I knew that Timmy had gone travelling for years on and off. What if Timmy and Lizzie had met up for old time's sake and she'd hit it off with his brother, only to end up married to him? I couldn't imagine why anyone would want to set themselves up like that, knowing they had a deep dark family secret that could potentially ruin everything if it had ever been found out.

"Let's say Timmy and Lizzie really do have that kind of past together... Will was here helping to search. It does rather suggest that this is exactly what it looks like, but it also suggests that Will knows about it."

"Or, he just knows something about it. Lizzie might not have told him the whole truth," Auryn said.

"And perhaps Lizzie wanted it to stay that way... but Timmy wouldn't keep his mouth shut," I finished.

"Or maybe Will did find out very recently and decided to take a little revenge on his brother," Auryn jumped in.

"Well! It's like being in a room with two criminal masterminds," Officer Kelly piped up. I turned to look and discovered that, although she'd said it in joking tones, she looked pretty disturbed.

"Let's look through the rest of the will. Perhaps that will tell us something more."

By the end of it, I was no more sure of anything than I had been at the start. What Jon had claimed Timmy had spouted at the barbecue had obviously had some basis in the truth. Timmy had bequeathed a sizeable sum of money to

Sally Marsden to be kept in trust for her until she was twenty one. I would imagine that as she'd been signed away for adoption, it was a pretty irregular request, but the document looked official and a lawyer's headed paper had been used - although it wasn't a firm I recognised.

I thought back to the day of the murder when Auryn and I had come to find out why Timmy hadn't turned up at the meeting. The door had been unlocked when we'd arrived and I knew Will and Lizzie didn't have a key. Had Timmy let them in, only to be betrayed? But that didn't mesh with the way we'd found his body. I was still completely clueless.

"It looks like rain."

I raised my head from the legal documents and saw that Auryn was looking outside of the glass doors. He'd left them open to let in cool air because the day had been a muggy one. Now I watched as fat splashes of rain started to fall on the patio, just as Auryn had said.

"Ethan's still out in his hot tub. I guess he's already wet," my fiancé said with a shrug. He turned back and noticed we were both watching him with curiosity. "What?"

"Nothing, it's just... this is quite the bombshell," I told him.

"I know that, but that's what the police are for." He smiled and inclined his head in Officer Kelly's direction.

"Of course," I said, handing the documents over to Officer Kelly. "Don't forget the photo..." I looked at the picture and the name on the back. I couldn't help but wonder if this was the child's adopted mother? It would make sense...

"I'm sure this will be an excellent lead. I'll pass on to Detective Gregory just how helpful you both were," Officer Kelly assured us, reverting to her professional persona.

"Thank you," I replied. It would be great to have a good word put in with law enforcement. Perhaps it would persuade Detective Gregory to overlook my past oversights.

I waited until Officer Kelly had left before I turned to Auryn with a quizzical look on my face.

"Don't look at me like that. It is a police matter!"

"But aren't you curious?" I pressed.

Auryn shot me a serious look. "Of course I am, but we can't lose sight of the fact that a man was murdered, right here." He pointed to the spot on the floor where the body had been. "And the information that we've just found out might have been what got him killed. We don't want to get in over our heads."

I looked down at the empty floor and then back up at Auryn. "I think we already are."

10

THE CHAMELEON

When I texted Tiff to let her know I was returning to Avery Zoo with dog food, she messaged back to tell me she'd gone over to The Lucky Zoo and had taken Rameses with her. I asked Auryn to drop me off at my zoo and then I hefted a 15kg sack of dog chow up the side of the large hill, before practically rolling down the other side. By the time I found Tiff, I was sweaty and probably smelled of dog food. That made me less than impressed to see my best friend and the man I was paying good money to be working right this second hanging around, shooting the breeze.

At least Rameses was happy to see me. He bounded right up and sniffed at me eagerly. I guess I really did smell of dog food…

"Hey Madi, how's it going?" Pierce said, looking incredibly relaxed for a man I'd just caught slacking off big time.

"I'm fine thank you, Pierce. What are you up to?" I meant it as a hint but it either sailed straight over his head, or he chose to ignore it. I'd have bet on the latter.

"I'm talking to this wonderful lady about our forthcoming

marketing and PR plans. It won't be long before we're the most popular zoo in the country. Then there's just the rest of the world to beat." He winked at Tiff when he said it. I ground my teeth in frustration. Trust Mr Smoothy Pierce to be able to claim work when I was certain his motives were anything but.

"What plans would those be?" I asked, determined to show him that I cared about what he was doing. Especially when he wasn't actually doing it.

"I'll feed Rameses. I think he needs it, the poor boy," Tiff said, sensing a showdown and behaving tactfully, as she always did. As it turned out, Rameses would have to wait a little longer to be fed.

Detective Alex Gregory must have left the station as soon as Officer Kelly had handed over our findings.

"Ms Amos, I need to ask you some questions..." he began. He stopped walking when he saw Pierce, who was in the midst of smiling at Tiff and had just reached out to brush a hair back from her face.

I felt time standstill as Alex Gregory's calm demeanour struggled with the rage I saw boiling behind his eyes. Rage directed at my marketing and PR genius.

"Tiff, might I have a word with you in private?" Detective Gregory said, apparently forgetting about the important questions he'd been about to ask me.

"Sure!" Tiff said and started to walk over to the detective.

"Hey now, hold up! Is she in some kind of trouble?" Pierce asked, stepping forwards and practically squaring up to the detective. I believed I'd got the measure of Pierce over the past week. I knew he wasn't seriously asking if Tiff was in trouble with the police, he'd just figured out that Detective Gregory had eyes on the same woman he did.

"It's a private matter," the detective said, his nostrils flaring a little.

"It's fine, Pierce," Tiff said, smiling at my employee and then at the detective. I knew she was trying to be fair to them both, but I could sense that trouble was now unavoidable.

"Well, if I'm not going to get a moment alone... Tiff, I'd really like us to become exclusive," Detective Gregory said, turning to fully face my beautiful friend. "I've never met anyone like you and I'll never forgive myself if I let you pass me by."

"I..." Tiff looked from Detective Gregory to Pierce and back again before she looked helplessly at me. I knew my best friend very well indeed. I'd known a day ago, when we'd spoken about her suitors, which one she was leaning towards, and I suspected where her heart lay - even though she might not be sure herself. However, Tiff was not one for confrontation, unless forced. And that was going to make this whole thing go south.

"Ha! Don't compete where you can't, Detective," Pierce said with a patronising smile. "I can offer her more than you dream of."

"I'm the detective for the Gigglesfield police force. And I know exactly what kind of man you are!" The detective answered the smile with a disparaging look.

"You have no idea," Pierce told him and there was danger in his voice. I woke up from my fascination at the battle beginning in front of me to wonder about Pierce all over again. Other than a couple of references, who could have been anyone really, I had no idea who my head of marketing and PR was. Was he about to show his true colours?

Detective Gregory turned to look at Pierce and there was something in his gaze that seemed to say *just try me, you don't know me either*. Pierce raised one dark eyebrow but to my intense surprise, he didn't open his mouth again.

"Madi, I need some time to ask those questions now," the detective said. His lapse into informality was the only sign I had that he was unfocused, perhaps even rattled. I merely nodded and then gestured that we should walk towards the barn conversion.

"You've got to be joking about him," I heard Pierce say right before we walked out of earshot.

Detective Alex Gregory froze in his tracks. Then he turned around.

"Detective..." I tried to say, but he was already striding back towards Tiff and Pierce.

"Oh-ho! Back for another round?" Pierce said with a grin and then ducked the roundhouse punch aimed at his ear.

"Have you gone mad?" I shouted after the detective.

Pierce landed first hit with a short straight jab to the nose that made Detective Gregory shake his head to refocus. "And don't try to do me for assault, either. You hit first," Pierce said, still shooting his mouth off.

"Stop this at once!" Tiff said moving forwards and then backing right up again when fists started flying.

As with the majority of fights, this one ended with both men on the floor, rolling around in the dirt. Fortunately for Tiff and me, fights aren't exactly silent. It wasn't long before some of my zoo staff had gathered, and I felt able to safely act. With a few swift instructions from me, some of my burlier keepers managed to pull the two men apart. Detective Gregory had a bloody nose and Pierce had a cut across the top of his right eyebrow. Both of them were covered in dust and were, in my mind, utterly ridiculous.

"You will not fight in my zoo. This is a family friendly place," I informed them. "I want both of you to leave the premises right now. Pierce, come back in tomorrow. Detective Gregory, I will answer your questions down at the station." Both men looked back at me with challenges in their eyes. I eyeballed them right back. This was my turf and I made the rules.

In the end, Detective Gregory's common sense prevailed. He threw one last pained look at Tiff and then walked away through the zoo towards the hill. Pierce watched him go with a self-satisfied smirk on his face, before I cleared my throat and pointed him in that direction too, as he'd apparently forgotten the way out.

For a moment, I missed the security team who'd been present at the zoo when I'd worked here as a consultant. But then I remembered what their main purpose had been, and the way I'd been lied to. The only thing I was grateful to them for was scaring off any future animal activists from trying to free the elephants, or other animals for that matter. Donald Trunk's unfortunate killing of an activist, alongside the arrest and interrogation of all but one of the others present, was a pretty stark warning that the zoo took the protection of its animals seriously. Although the security was now long gone, no one had ever come back.

I watched as Pierce trudged off and was about to turn away when he muttered something.

"Never wanted this anyway…" he grumbled, just within my hearing. Whilst Pierce really needed to work harder at not being overheard saying things that got him in trouble, it alarmed me all over again, feeding my paranoia that Pierce was really a spy, told to get the job and then helped by a hidden team to make it appear that he was good at his task. Similar things had happened before, and I didn't feel completely crazy for wondering again…

"Madi, I'm not sure if this is a good time…"

I looked around to find Gabby standing by my side with a hopeful look on her face. I thought about the questions I needed to answer down at the station and I thought about Detective Gregory's unprofessional behaviour at my zoo. He could wait ten more minutes.

"What's up?" I asked, smiling at my newest keeper whilst

secretly hoping it wasn't bad news. There'd been enough of that today already.

"At the arts and crafts day, I spoke to some of the people from Avery Zoo when they came across for the judging. They said at Avery, everyone can submit ideas for events and then the events get put on. Is that right?" she asked.

I tilted my head from side to side. "More or less. Auryn lets staff submit event ideas but, if approved, that member of staff, or group, must then put together the event themselves. Staff are encouraged to help one another out, but it's about being responsible for your own ideas and finding a way to make them successful."

Gabby nodded. "Okay. In that case... could I put on a creepy crawly day? I'd love to get visitors handling some of the animals I look after, and I also think there could be talks on caring for reptiles, amphibians, and insects. It would be great!"

I considered it. "Who do you think might be interested in attending the event?"

"Everyone! The animals I look after are great."

I smiled but shook my head. "You have to remember that while you are incredibly passionate about the animals you care for, not everyone feels the same way. If I might, an angle to pursue might be 'conquering your fears'. Another idea might be promoting the event to children, who are fascinated by things they believe are 'gross'."

"But they're not gross!" Gabby protested.

"That's exactly what you'll show them... once they've turned up to see some gross animals." I thought about it again. "Babies are also great for getting interest. I bet lots of people would like to see the baby chameleons and hold them when they're a little bigger. Just so long as it doesn't stress the animals out..." I never advocated prolonged periods of animals being forced on display or handed around. It was unfair on the animal - great or small.

"Those ideas do sound like smart ones. Maybe I could talk to Vanessa about it. Do you know if she's already put on an event like that at Avery Zoo?"

"I don't think so. She's happier with insects than people." It wasn't meant as an insult. That was just the way Avery's creepy crawly keeper was.

"Do you want to help me sort the chameleons? Some of them have been growing really fast. I could do with a pair of extra hands."

I could tell that Gabby was doing everything she could to rebuild our relationship after chameleon-gate - as I now liked to think of it. I decided that Detective Gregory could wait another ten minutes or so before he questioned me.

"How much do you know about the collection you've got here?" Gabby asked smiling kindly when we walked into the creepy crawly house.

"When this zoo was set up, the plans for the animals had mostly already been done. However, thanks to the work I did at Snidely Safari, I was able to make a few changes that I thought made sense. The original plans for this zoo were made six years ago. You won't believe how much changes in that time. Anyway, I also benefited from a better knowledge of appropriate enclosures, again, thanks to Snidely." I had gotten uncomfortably close to some of the snakes during my consultation work there. It had definitely influenced my decision to not include any highly venomous snakes in The Lucky Zoo's collection. I knew that the scarier the snake, the more it drew people in, but I also knew that accidents and escapes happened. That was why I'd vetoed a few of the flashier ideas that the Abraham family had listed on their original plans. Now I feared that Gabby was about to tell me just how boring those choices were.

"You've got a really good range of animals. You know I'm a chameleon and reptile expert, and I'd love to bring more of those in, but I'm really happy with what you have, and the enclosures you've made. I would love to add a breeding wing in the future, which you'll need extra enclosures for, but yeah - it's great. I was interested as to who had set it up in the first place and now I know."

"You don't think it's boring?" I said, deciding to voice my worry aloud.

Gabby shook her head. "No! I know you get the fear factor with something like a black mamba, but these animals are all pretty deadly little hunters themselves - just, on a small scale," she said, when I must have looked alarmed.

We walked to the behind the scenes area and she hefted out the tank containing the tiny chameleons. "We'd better get sorting these! Only a couple of months until they'll all need their own separate enclosures." She looked up at me and grinned. "Better start talking to some other zoos!"

I nodded and then gently stuck my hand into the enclosure, letting a tiny green chameleon onto my finger.

"Did you know it's mostly a myth that chameleons change their colours to blend in with their environment?"

"I did know that," I said with a little smile. Before working at Snidely, I'd done a lot of reptile research, but it had all been fairly generic. "Is it something to do with emotional states instead?"

"That's one of the things that can affect it! Their markings and colouration are also influenced by the chameleons health, temperature, and their surroundings, too," she added with an answering smile. "They like living in trees, so although the size of the enclosure is good at the moment for these babies that my own pair had, if you decide we should keep a couple, it would be great to have an enclosure which mostly consists of trees. We could be creative about how we build it…" Gabby stopped talking and smiled at me. "Sorry, getting a bit carried away again, wasn't I?"

I looked kindly at the keeper who loved the animals she cared for with a passion. "You can get as carried away as you like. As long as you talk to me before putting any major plans in action, I'll most likely say yes. I trust your judgement. This area of the zoo is yours. I only want to remain informed." I really did like to give keepers a free rein as much as they wanted. I was a firm believer that the people closest to the animals they looked after knew what was best for them the majority of the time. Sometimes it helped to have an outsider to bounce ideas about with - which was mostly what my consulting work consisted of - but for the most part, the keepers knew best. I only wanted to be there to play devil's advocate to make sure that they really had thought everything through.

"Thanks! This is the best job I've ever had," Gabby told me.

"That makes my day," I told her in return. Admittedly, something as little as a chocolate bar would have made my day given the day I was having, but I meant it all the same.

I excused myself, knowing that I was probably pushing my luck with Detective Gregory. I very much doubted he'd be in a good mood either.

My phone rang as I was walking up the hill. "All right, I'm coming…" I muttered, assuming it was the police station. I glanced at the screen and discovered it was Gloria from my publishers.

"Hi Madi, are you free this evening for dinner? I've got something important to discuss with you."

My mind immediately raced. Was it bad news? Was it bad that my mind had immediately jumped to bad news?

"We can go for dinner, my treat," Gloria continued. I tried

to decipher her words as to whether there was sympathy in them, but if there was, I couldn't hear it.

"I can do that," I said, remembering Auryn and I were supposed to be taking a few days off - first for the house cleaning and now, theoretically, to sort out the garden. He wouldn't be thrilled that I'd be skiving off dinner, but I never said no to food, especially not free food. "May I ask what it's about?"

"It's a surprise!" Gloria told me, completely infuriatingly.

I raised my eyebrows. That meant it probably wasn't bad news, unless my publisher was a complete sadist. 'Surprise! Everyone thinks your comics suck!' wasn't the kind of news you took someone out to dinner to give.

"I'll see you later," Gloria said, leaving me with questions and no answers. *As if I need any new mysteries in my life,* I thought with bemusement.

The next morning, Auryn woke me up by letting me know that Scarlett was coming over to collect Rameses. She'd apparently apologised for giving us the runaround, but she'd spoken to Ethan, and he'd agreed to keep Rameses with his dogs. Scarlett had decided that other canine company might cheer up the Pharaoh Hound. I privately thought that Rameses was doing just fine now that he and Lucky had reached a tenuous accord, and he'd enjoyed being at the zoo around people, but Scarlett was the dog's owner now, so Auryn had of course said we'd respect her wishes.

All the same, I couldn't keep from grumbling when we sat down to breakfast. My questioning session with Detective Gregory had been pretty dreadful. He'd been in such a foul mood I'd thought he might even try to reignite the tiny over-sight I'd made by not telling the police about the dog lead I'd found on the drive. I'd been very glad to get out of the police station a free woman. As for the murder case, the detective had agreed that the will was sufficient evidence to bring in Will and Lizzie Marsden for questioning. I was willing to bet the detective's sour mood would spread to them when they were brought back down south for questioning.

The meal with my publisher had turned out to be good news - at least, she'd thought it was good news. My comic's success had reached some ears in Hollywood and there was apparently a lot of interest around having a film made. When I'd questioned how they proposed to animate the comics - especially as they were more funny scenes than coherent storylines - I'd received the answer I'd dreaded ever since film making had been mentioned. The Hollywood people were interested in my story. They wanted to know the ins and outs of how *Monday's Menagerie* had risen to fame, and the mortal dramas in my own life that surrounded it (someone had clearly been doing their research!) I'd had to take a deep breath when Gloria had said all of that. My first reaction was to say no, absolutely not, but saying that would obviously lead to more questions - questions I couldn't answer. The problem was, most of the story behind my comic's success was protected by the Official Secrets Act, and I wasn't sure of how good an alternative story I could come up with.

Then there was the horror of having my own life displayed on the big screen. I'd never actually sought any limelight and the idea of some faux memoir made me itch with discomfort. In the end, I'd played for time by telling Gloria it was a really big opportunity and that I needed to think about it. After I'd got home, I'd called Katya and filled her in on the problem. She'd promised me that she'd either get back to me, or I'd find my problem had been solved by some behind-the-scenes persuasion. I'd known better than to ask beyond that, but with a bit of luck, the film was dead in the water.

"Are you okay to take Rameses over? He's taken to you," Auryn said.

The tan coloured dog had seemed to adopt me as his chosen person over the past day. He was currently leaning against my leg, watching mournfully as I ate my cornflakes. "No problem. If it weren't for my strong suspicion that Lucky is planning something dastardly beneath the facade of tolerance, I'd say we should offer to keep him ourselves. Especially as he seems to be causing Scarlett such inconvenience." I rolled my eyes when I said it, knowing that I was in safe company with Auryn.

"Maybe we should get a puppy?"

"You think?" I asked, entertaining the idea. I'd always treated Lucky like a dog with his lead walking training and the adventures I'd hoped to take him on when working as a consultant. *Adventures that were still going to happen,* I firmly reminded myself. But I could tell that while he loved Lucky, Auryn was a dog person at heart. His friendly, happy-go-lucky personality just fit with a dog's perfectly. At the same time, I had no doubt that I was a cat person, but I did also like dogs.

Rameses sighed and breathed doggy breath in my face. I shot him a 'do you have to?' look. Yep, I definitely preferred animals who understood the concept of personal space. "Hopefully you'll be all settled in with Scarlett before long," I told the dog, hoping I sounded surer than I felt. Much like myself, Scarlett did not actually strike me as a dog person.

When I pulled into the lane that led to the Marsden house, I suddenly realised my phone charger was missing from the

177

car. In a moment of clarity, I realised I must have left it behind when cleaning the house. When we'd found the will, everything had gone up in the air a little. Auryn had tidied the house some more, but I wasn't surprised to discover I'd forgotten something. Fortunately, I'd attached the house key Scarlett had given us to my main keyring, so I was able to let myself in when I pulled up. To my surprise, I heard movement inside of the house as soon as I opened the door.

"Hello?" I called, tightening my grip on Rameses' lead. The dog was happy to be home, but I didn't want him to run into an intruder - especially not when they could be none other than Timmy's murderer!

"Hello? Madi, is that you?" a familiar voice called down the stairs.

"What are you doing here?" I asked Officer Kelly in as light a way as I could.

She blushed all the same. "I'm just checking for anything else we might have missed. Detective Gregory wanted to make double sure now that this will has turned up. I've kept everything tidy," she added, keen to let me know she hadn't undone the hours of work we'd all put in yesterday.

"You didn't find anything?" I asked, but both of us knew there was no way anything had been missed. The police officer was here for a very different reason. She wasn't ready to let go.

"No, nothing. By the way, the Marsdens came back down this morning. Lizzie finally caved in and admitted she had come here that morning. No one answered the front door and it was apparently locked. She went round the side gate and across the patio and saw that her brother-in-law was dead. Then she claims she panicked and decided to leave, instead of reporting it to the police." Officer Kelly raised an eyebrow to show what she thought of that story. "Understandably, they're both being held in custody for now."

"Did she say why she came all the way down from Leeds?" I asked, surprised but pleased that my police officer friend was in such a sharing mood. I supposed it was probably because, although they thought they had a good murder suspect, some missing piece must still be eluding them.

"Her husband claims he had no idea she was gone. Apparently, she was supposed to be at work. When Lizzie saw the will, she stopped being so tight-lipped. We'd already managed to confirm her maiden name by then, so we knew she'd had the baby with Timothy Marsden." Officer Kelly sighed. "I thought she'd just admit she'd done it at that point, but she didn't. She said that everything she'd told us was true. Timmy had apparently called her on the day he'd changed his will, letting her know that he'd decided to pass on his part of the family inheritance to the child, should he die. She said that with anyone normal, it might not have been anything to worry about, but she knew Timmy was an adrenaline junkie. One slip on a mountain and she knew her husband would discover the terrible truth. Lizzie claims that she was visiting Timmy to reason with him to change the will and forget about the child. After all, they had given it up for adoption, so it wasn't theirs anymore - that's what she said anyway."

"But Will was in here searching with her. Doesn't that imply he already knew the truth?"

Officer Kelly nodded. "We thought of that, too. Lizzie was still begging us not to tell him at that point. She says she told her husband that they were searching for a will that cut him out of the family money, should Timmy die an early death. I've no idea how she justified why Timmy had called her with that news, rather than call his brother, or even told her at all, but she claims she managed to convince him it was the truth. Apparently, family tradition dictates that the family money is passed on only to Marsdens. Spouses get missed. It's blood over anything else I suppose. With that logic, the child would have every right to inherit, as they are a blood relation, but then - there never was supposed to be a child. Lizzie said it was a mistake that happened when she was young and foolish and Timmy had looser morals..."

I inwardly raised my eyebrows. After what I now knew about Timmy's morals, I wasn't sure I wanted to imagine that.

"It wasn't until years later when they met up for old time's sake that she also met his brother, Will, and things just happened from there." Officer Kelly shrugged. "It sounds to me like a motive for murder."

"I don't know..." I said, struggling to put it all together in my head. "I suppose the way Timmy was found does correspond with her coming in through the back door and stabbing him. Then she could have gone through and unlocked the front door to make the police think it happened a different way - breaking and entering." I thought some more. "Hey, did she say what time she thought she'd arrived?"

"She says it was around eleven."

"Did she see a dog lead on the ground?" I asked.

Officer Kelly frowned. "I'm not sure if that's been asked. Do you think it's relevant?"

"I don't know. Andy said he might have heard shouting. If he was right, then Timmy was still alive at that time. I suppose Lizzie might have killed him when she came along later, but don't you think it's something to look into? He might have been shouting on the phone... or anything... but it could help."

"I'll make a note to get that question asked." Officer Kelly looked around the kitchen we were standing in with a wistful expression. "It's stupid, I know, now that I know everything he was up to, but I'll miss him."

"I know," I said, understandingly. I might see Timmy as a bit of an ass, but he'd obviously had a way of connecting with those he had dalliances with in a caring way. I thought that both Officer Kelly and Annabelle Wright might have got closer to ending up with Timmy than I'd originally imagined. Not all flings were equal.

I bit my lip when I remembered something else that Annabelle Wright's husband had said. It had bothered me the other day when we'd come in to clean. "Andy Wright said he heard classic rock playing when he came round and then left without seeing Timmy, but the CD in the sound system is pop music. I had a look, but I couldn't even see a classic rock CD around." It was really beginning to bug me.

"Maybe it was one of the neighbours' music?"

I thought about that and then nodded. "It could have been Ethan's radio. He was playing music when I let Rameses out before he disappeared. I think he likes to listen to music while he sits in his hot tub," I explained, realising that I'd always heard some kind of music when I'd been outside. He'd even been asked to turn the music down when we were all out for a barbecue.

"Lizzie Marsden probably thought that was a gift from heaven. It was all the sound cover she needed to kill her brother-in-law and get away with it. It's just too bad we haven't been able to find the murder weapon."

"Hmmm," I said, feeling the cogs turning in my head. I looked down at Rameses and he looked back up at me. I suddenly had the strong feeling that the mystery of how Rameses had got out, and then back in, might just be the final piece in the puzzle that uncovered the murderer. "I don't think Lizzie Marsden killed Timmy," I announced, remembering something else. It hadn't seemed significant at the time but now it had risen to the surface and seemed to make the whole thing glaringly obvious. "When I let Rameses outside, I noticed there was water on the floor of the kitchen. I didn't put much thought into where it had come from. I suppose I explained it away as being Rameses, but he isn't a drooler." It was one of the things I'd been glad to learn when the dog had stayed with us. "Perhaps there were water marks on the patio, too, but they'd have dried quicker in the sun."

"There wasn't any water on the floor when I got here. It would have been logged by the first responders, too."

"Perhaps it dried up, or perhaps..." The final piece of the puzzle dropped into place. "Someone could have come back when Auryn and I went outside to call the police. They could have wiped up the evidence that they'd ever been inside the house. Only... they left the gate between properties open and Rameses got out. That was how he got away! I wouldn't be surprised if Rameses came back in that way, too. Heinrich was making a racket when Auryn and I came to confront Will and Lizzie. Rameses must have used it to find his way back home. The culprit would have felt pressured into letting him back through in order to perpetuate the idea that Rameses jumped the fence - even though he'd never done it before."

I shook my head. "It was the killer's final mistake. Ethan Pleasant was listening to everything that I'd been talking about with Georgina, and then Harry, on the day I'd come to look for Rameses. He'd have known that the prevailing theory was that Rameses had jumped the fence, so logically, he should be able to jump back over. He must have let Rameses back through the gate when he turned up again and probably got Heinrich sniffing around exactly where he didn't want him. If he'd just kept him in the garden and then told us he'd found him, the side gate theory would have looked a lot more likely. I think he thought he was being smart but really, he panicked."

I rubbed my chin thoughtfully. "Ethan said he was in the hot tub when the murder must have happened, but I heard the sounds of splashing when Auryn and I arrived. If that were true, he'd have been in there for hours!"

"Well, it was a nice day," Officer Kelly allowed, playing devil's advocate.

"Sure, but it would also be the perfect way to wash off any evidence that you just murdered your next door neighbour."

"But why on earth would this next door neighbour want to kill Timmy?"

"Don't you remember? We found that gym membership card with Shona Pleasant's name on it. Ethan must have discovered, like a lot of men, that his wife was having an affair with Timmy Marsden. He must have been the first to act upon it," I said.

"That's all well and good, but without a murder weapon or any physical evidence - which you think was deliberately removed - we've got nothing on him. Just an escaped dog and the knowledge that his wife was probably cheating. Even that could be explained away. She could have popped round for a cup of tea and forgotten her gym card."

I snorted to show what I thought of *that* theory, but I knew Officer Kelly had a point. We were stuck, and as it stood, I thought the police were far more likely to go with the couple who'd been caught red-handed, searching the house, and who also had witness testimony placing Lizzie in the area on the day of the murder - when she should have been hundreds of miles away.

"Someone had better do something," I said aloud. I looked down at the dog. "I'm supposed to be delivering Rameses to Ethan right now. I'm sure he won't mind a friendly chat at the same time..."

"Madi, don't do anything dangerous," my police officer friend begged me.

"Ethan has no quarrel with me that I know of. Anyway, you'll be right behind the hedgerow, recording everything he

RUBY LOREN

says and ready to jump into action at a moment's notice. What could possibly go wrong?"

"I suppose it's not the worst idea in the world…" Officer Kelly mused.

But it turned out that it was. It really was.

"Ethan, are you around?" I called over the hedge, and then peered over the gate.

The man I believed was a killer turned around in his hot tub and smiled at me before lifting a hand in greeting. "Come on through! My two dogs stay inside, apart from when we go for walks, but I'm sure they'll be happy to have a new friend. He'll have to stay in, too, unfortunately. I don't have the fences for it, especially when he seems to like running off." He pushed himself up out of the water, displaying an enviable six pack. Working in tech seemed to leave you a lot of time for relaxing and working out - or at least, it did in Ethan's case.

"I'm sure Rameses will be just fine until Scarlett can make arrangements for him to live with her."

Ethan wrapped a towel around himself and then ran a hand through his dark hair. "You think so? I got the impression she was just farming him off on anyone she could until she can get round to selling him."

"Selling him?" I asked, momentarily distracted from the mission at hand.

"He's quite a valuable dog. I should know. It was all Timmy ever talked about." Ethan offered me a sad smile, which I returned, trying to remember the game I was playing. "He's some kind of high-end pedigree. Timmy always said that a breeder would pay through the nose for him to breed with their bitches. I'm guessing they'd pay more than

184

that to keep him. He cost a fair packet to begin with." Ethan shrugged. "My little guys are rescues. Between you and me, I always thought Timmy bought him as a status symbol more than anything else. He never hunted with him, and then he left him behind when he went on holiday and paid for the housekeeper to come in more often. That's not the life a dog should have!"

"No, it's not," I agreed, making a mental note to have a word with Scarlett Marsden when all was done and dusted.

It was with some reluctance that I turned the conversation towards the confession I hoped to get from Ethan Pleasant. Although I certainly didn't condone murder or anyone who committed it, on the face of things, I found I liked Ethan. If Timmy had been alive and you'd set both men together and asked me to pick the one I'd like to hang out with, I'd have chosen the man with whom I was currently sharing company. But if he was the murderer I suspected he was... then he needed to be brought to justice, no matter how pleasant Ethan Pleasant might appear to be on the surface.

"You know, if Rameses hadn't got out, I might not have realised you were in Timmy Marsden's garden on the day that he died," I said, unable to find a better way to ease in.

Ethan's happy expression vanished. "I'm sorry? I didn't go into his garden at all that day, not even when the police arrived. I walked around the front to see what had happened. Anyway, you know Rameses jumped the fence. He must have jumped it when he came back, too."

"Originally, I thought that was the case. Then I spoke to Scarlett and she said that in all the time they'd had Rameses, he'd never jumped over the fence before. It just doesn't seem very likely that he'd suddenly jump over something that had kept him in prior to that. Well - not twice in a row anyway. I had thought that he must have got out through the side gate after all, but when he appeared in the garden a second time, I should have put it together. You let him out accidentally when you came back through the gate to wipe up the water you must have realised you'd left on the floor, and then you let him back in when he came back, because the dog he knew was out in the garden."

Ethan's face was ashen. "You don't have anything," he hissed, so quietly I was sure that Officer Kelly wasn't going to have picked it up.

"We found your wife's gym membership card in the house. I assume you knew she was cheating, which was the reason why you killed Timmy. You must have watched him bring back countless women, but it was a different story when he took a fancy to Shona..."

Ethan laughed but it was a humourless sound. "I don't suppose you bothered to look at the dates on that gym card? My wife hasn't gone near a gym in an age. She crash diets these days. I thought working out was something we would bond doing, but that went down the toilet like everything else. You just found that card's final resting place, but believe me, it was a long time ago." He shrugged. "I've known about it for what feels like forever. "Shona married me as soon as I was someone. Back then, I was high on money and success. I didn't realise she was a gold digger. Now, I'm a different man, and in case you hadn't noticed, she doesn't live here anymore. We're all but divorced in name."

"So, that's not why you killed Timmy?" Now I was completely lost.

Ethan's eyes glittered. "Of course not. Not that I did kill him." The tiny smile on his lips made me believe he realised he was being recorded. I should have expected that level of paranoia from a man who'd made his money in technology.

"Why did you do it?" I pressed, hoping he'd at least give me an idea, even if it wasn't an incriminating one. "Was he damaging your business? Did you fall out over the loud music?" I was really reaching here.

Ethan shook his head, looking amused. "Hypothetically, Timmy got what was coming to him. You know what he was like. He should never have been on the list for The Lords of the Downs - and certainly not ahead of me."

I couldn't believe it. All along, it had been about the stupid club! "And when he died, that meant you were next in line," I said, remembering what Harry had said, loudly and inappropriately right after Timmy had died. "Why do you care so much?"

"Don't you see? Timmy was offered a place because his family has old money that they passed down through generations. He hadn't done anything remotely impressive with his life, but he was still invited to join the club, just because. By comparison, I came from nothing to gain more wealth and success than most of those so-called successful members earn in a lifetime. But still, I was bumped along and moved down the list until they just couldn't overlook me anymore. With Timmy gone, I'll accept my place in the club and finally get some recognition around here." He shook his head. "Hypothetically, of course," he added.

Even though I assumed that none of this would count as evidence, I hoped that Officer Kelly was getting it all. At least they'd know who they had to try to pin it on and they could let the innocent-ish couple go.

"This all goes back to your school days, doesn't it? You were at the state school and they were at the private one. There was rivalry between the two schools and your peers, but you've taken it to a whole new level."

"There's always been this prejudice against me. Even when I became what I am now! It's ridiculous." Ethan looked furious for the first time. I'd hit a nerve all right.

"You were clever about it, too. You knew there had to be

evidence, and what better than a handy hot tub with its chlorine-treated water to get rid of the blood you'd got on you?" I said, looking across at the heated jacuzzi. "What happened to the knife? Hypothetically of course." I couldn't resist adding the sarcastic comment.

To my surprise, Ethan walked over to the patch of calla lilies growing in the marshy soil around the jacuzzi and rummaged around. I followed him out of curiosity and stood by the tub. A second later, he picked up a nasty looking kitchen knife. "It might have had too much blood on it for the tub, but a bucket of soapy water mixed with bleach took care of that. When you have as much land as this, who's going to notice you pour a little water away?" He looked contemplatively from the knife to me.

"Don't," I said, knowing what he was thinking. Ethan assumed I'd come alone to hand over the dog, and had then foolishly decided to come across and accuse him of murder. He might suspect that I was recording the conversation, but I doubted he suspected the presence of anyone else. After all, the police were interviewing the Marsdens, and I knew how well gossip spread in this town. There was no way Ethan would have expected there to be a police officer in his next door neighbour's house - having let herself in with a key she shouldn't have possessed. That was why he now thought he might be able to get away with murder... twice.

"Maybe you're right. You're like me. You were a nobody, and now you're not. If anything were to happen to either of us you can guarantee there'd be a lot of interest." He flipped the knife around, looking worryingly at ease with it. I wondered if, as well as a strict gym regime, Ethan had taken some kind of knife handling class. If there was such a thing, I was willing to bet Ethan had heard of it.

He looked back at me. "But then again... you seem to be

the only one who's strung it all together. No one else is looking my way, and I'd like it to stay that way."

"You'd be making a mistake," I said, still clinging to the barrier I hoped my fame had erected around me.

He shrugged. "I wouldn't have got where I am today without making a gamble or two."

That was when I knew he'd made up his mind and the coin had fallen on the wrong side for me.

I backed away, but Ethan was no slouch. He flipped the knife back into his hand and darted forwards. In a loud burst of barking, Rameses lunged to meet him. In my shock, I let go of his lead and could then only watch as the dog jumped to meet the man with the knife.

"No!" I shouted, running forwards myself, in an effort to see the dog unharmed. He'd done nothing to deserve any of this.

But luck favoured Rameses and he missed the blade. Ethan turned at the last moment and the dog merely scraped his arm with his teeth, before overshooting. I was not going to be afforded as lucky an escape. Running towards a man wielding a terrifying knife when you had nothing to defend yourself with was hardly a recipe for success.

"Officer Kelly!" I shouted, as I tried to put the brakes on but felt myself slide on the mud that surrounded the jacuzzi. Instinct made me grasp for Ethan as I slipped, and for one hopeful moment, I held his right wrist and managed to wrangle it away from my face. The next second we were falling sideways over the side of the tub. My elbow hit the bumpy interior with a nasty bang. The pain made me open my mouth and for a second water rushed in. I disentangled myself from Ethan and pushed upwards, my drive for oxygen overpowering any last remaining logic that told me to hang fast to that knife-wielding hand.

I inhaled and then coughed before rolling back over the

side of the jacuzzi and landing on the grass with a wet squelch. I did some more spluttering and crawled away from the tub, hoping to put some distance between myself and my attacker before he inevitably struck again. Officer Kelly rushed up the garden towards me, and I felt a flash of relief. She had her truncheon out. It wasn't a knife, but at least it might give her a fighting chance.

"What happened?" Officer Kelly asked, looking at me in alarm. Rameses rushed over and began washing my face.

I managed to push myself upright, using the arm that hadn't made contact with the tub, and turned around.

Ethan was nowhere to be seen.

"He must have hit his head and gone under!" I said, realising that my attacker hadn't resurfaced.

Officer Kelly stood by my side and looked at the tub. She didn't make a move, and for a second I saw a dark thought flash across her face.

"You've got to pull him out," I told her. "He needs to face justice. But be careful, he was holding a knife," I added, just in case. But I didn't believe Ethan had kept hold of it. He may even have inflicted some damage to himself. The whirling jets of water made it hard to tell, but the water still appeared the same blue of the tub's lining.

After turning off the jets so she could see, Officer Kelly reached into the tub and managed to haul Ethan's upper body out of the water. Then, between us, we got him onto the grass and into recovery position. I patted his back, hoping it would be enough. I wasn't sure if I was willing to perform mouth to mouth on a man who'd just tried to kill me. I did my best to be a good citizen, but surely that was pushing it.

A second later, he coughed, and up came all of the water he'd swallowed. It was enough for Officer Kelly, who snapped a pair of handcuffs on him.

"Ethan Pleasant, you are under arrest for the murder of Timothy Marsden. You do not have to say anything, but it may harm your defence if you do not mention when questioned something which you later rely on in court. Anything you do say may be given in evidence." Officer Kelly looked up at me when she'd finished giving him his rights. "I alerted the station as soon as I heard things go south across the hedge. They'll be here any moment now," she told me.

I nodded and experimented moving my arm. Nothing seemed to be broken but I was willing to bet there'd be a big bruise to go with the story I'd have to tell. Rameses fawned around my legs and looked up at me with big puppy-dog eyes.

"Believe me, you'll be getting a treat when this is all over," I promised him.

I was certain that Rameses' leap at Ethan had saved my life, whilst endangering his own. The logical part of my animal-tuned brain said that the dog hadn't been trying to attack Ethan, he'd merely thought we were all playing a game - but I was grateful all the same. The thought of having unwittingly put an animal at risk horrified me, but I also thought it might just be bringing me round to the arguments dog people had spouted for so long. They really were man and woman's best friend.

"If Scarlett really does want to get rid of you, there'll always be a home for you with me," I promised the dog. "And heck, if she wants paying, I've got plenty to spare."

11

A DANGEROUS GAME

uryn came to find me at the police station. One of the police officers had offered to look at my elbow, but beyond a scrape I hadn't realised the fall had caused, they'd deemed it merely badly bruised. The same could apparently be said for Ethan Pleasant. He'd been taken to hospital as a precaution, but right after I'd finished answering questions I'd seen him being led into the station.

"What happened?" My fiancé asked when he blazed through the door. I explained in as few words as possible how I'd finally pieced everything together, and how it had seemed like a totally safe and sensible idea to try to get a confession out of Ethan whilst covertly recording it. I'd thought we were being clever but recent events had shown the opposite was true.

"I wish you weren't so gung-ho," Auryn bemoaned.

"I wish I wasn't either," I agreed wholeheartedly.

"Well done Rameses for saving your life," Auryn said, giving the dog a good scratch behind the ears. I hadn't let go of him since I'd picked up his lead right after Ethan had come to.

"I think we should adopt him. You want a dog and... well, he deserves it. Any pet that is brave enough to save its owner's life deserves a good home."

"What about Lucky?"

"Lucky's not scared or stressed by him. I know they fight, but what siblings don't? I don't see why, with a bit of work, they can't get on." I knew I didn't need to say anymore. Hope had ignited in Auryn's eyes as soon as I'd mentioned adopting the dog.

"I thought Scarlett was keeping him?" he asked.

"It might not be true, but Ethan seemed to think she wasn't going to. He thought she might want to sell him because he's supposed to be worth something."

"I'll call her right now," Auryn announced and then shot me a worried look. "That is, if you're okay to be on your own for a bit?"

"Who's on their own? I've got Rameses," I told him with a wan smile. "Anyway, I've been through worse than this little scrape."

"I know you have," Auryn said, sounding more tired than I felt. And I felt pretty darn tired.

"I'm just looking forward to lunch," I muttered to myself. Auryn looked back at me and rolled his eyes to show he'd heard. He finished it with a grin, and then Scarlett must have answered the phone because he turned and walked away to find someplace quieter.

In his absence, Detective Alex Gregory walked out into the foyer where I was sitting, waiting to be released.

He made a beeline for me. "I believe that I have you to thank for realising that Ethan Pleasant was our man, although, I still can't say I'm sure on the motive behind it all," the detective began.

"You and me both."

"I'm glad you worked it out, however, it is my duty to

advise you that these things are best left to the police. You risked a lot when you decided to confront him over it. Officer Kelly Lane has been informed that she should never have let you proceed with your plan." He eyeballed me. "I'm not actually quite clear on why she was there in the first place..."

I deliberately looked away. If Officer Kelly wanted to tell him the truth she could. If she'd made up a story, then I thought she should be responsible for that, too.

"Anyway, all's well that ends well," he finished, surprising me into turning back. When I looked at him he smiled, and I thought I could see why Tiff had started to fall for the police detective.

"You haven't given up on her, have you?" Up until now, my conversation with Detective Gregory had been strictly about the murder with me giving an exact account of what had happened between Ethan Pleasant and me, but now I felt the need to help him out on a more personal level.

"I haven't... I don't know," the detective confessed, sitting down next to me with a frown on his face. "That other guy seemed so sure of himself. Maybe he's right and he is the better man for Tiff. I feel like an idiot for fighting with him."

I snorted, causing him to turn and stare at me. "Pierce works in marketing, although, between you and me, he's more of a salesman. Of course he's going to give you the impression that he's exactly what Tiff needs. Selling things and creating the right impression is what he does for a living! Believe me, I've been on the receiving end of it."

I hadn't forgotten the way that Pierce had managed to net himself the job. I didn't have any qualms now he'd amply demonstrated that he was up to the job, but that didn't mean I wasn't aware of the way all things Pierce worked. And from what I'd seen this past week, Detective Gregory was the horse I wanted to back in the race for Tiff's heart.

Pierce might be a perfectly nice man, but he smacked of the same self-confident men Tiff had come unstuck with before. It was often only this type of man who was brave enough to approach a woman as stunning as my best friend, which in turn was why she ended up with so many terrible men. I didn't sense any of that overinflated self-importance in the detective. I knew it was very early days yet, but I thought he might be a man with mileage. I didn't want him to drop at the first hurdle.

"I'd better do something about it, hadn't I? Rather than moping around like a fool."

"You have my approval," I joked, lightening the mood.

"In that case, I'll go and find her right away." The detective stood up and then hesitated. "After this murder case is tied up that is. I got a bit carried away for a moment there."

"Good luck, Detective."

"I think I'll need it in all aspects of my life. We may have a murder weapon, a motive, and an idea as to how it was all done, but the knife looks to be completely clean, and a motive as stupid as the one you say Ethan gave you sounds rather implausible," the detective confided in a hushed tone.

"But what about the recording Officer Kelly made on her phone?"

The detective sighed. "Yes, about that... when she reached over to pull Ethan out of the jacuzzi, it fell out of her pocket. We collected it and gave it to our resident tech expert, but she doesn't think she can do anything at all with it. Technology has its downfalls doesn't it?"

"It certainly does," I agreed, thinking of the man currently sat in a holding cell, waiting to be interrogated for murder. Unfortunately, I was inclined to agree with Detective Gregory that it was going to be a hard slog getting Ethan Pleasant convicted for murder. Even though we now all knew for certain he'd done it, convincing a jury would be another matter. Not only did the police have to fight against the flaws that Detective Gregory had just listed, they would also be going up against the best legal help Ethan Pleasant's money could buy, and I knew he could buy a lot.

I sighed out loud when I was once more sitting alone in the foyer. I would be called up to testify. It wasn't something I enjoyed doing. I also knew that this time would probably be the worst yet, as the media were sure to get wind of it. When you added Ethan's fairly well-known name into the mix, it made it that much worse.

It was funny how in my head I did everything I could to stay out of the limelight, but in reality, everything I did seemed to constitute another press opportunity. *Perhaps I should just accept it and let them make this ridiculous film about me!* I thought to myself, wondering if I chose to embrace the fame, it would go away. People spent their entire lives chasing it. "And here I am trying to beat it off with a stick. Maybe that's where I'm going wrong," I said to myself.

One week later, life seemed to have settled back to its normal pace. My biggest worry was discussing a menu for the restaurant with my brand new chef, Connie Breeze, and figuring out wedding plans. As the restaurant was now officially able to serve food, and had been certified to do so, with the help of Connie, Auryn and I had finally decided on a date for the big day. We were going to be married on October 15th. It was a date that was just far enough from Halloween that, although the autumn colours would be around, our zoo Halloween events wouldn't be in full swing, and it was long enough after summer that the school holiday rush would be well over. There should be nothing at all to worry about apart from the wedding itself.

I was busy writing names on wedding invitations when there was a knock on the front door. Rameses got to his feet and padded out to see who it was. I watched him go for a moment before following. It somehow amused me to see how laid back he was when it came to who was at the door. He wasn't a dog who barked a lot. It made me all the more certain that when he'd jumped at Ethan, it hadn't been out of malice. It might be nice to believe he'd recognised his master's killer and had risen to my defence, but I was happy with Rameses just being a normal dog - not some canine superhero.

When Auryn had contacted Scarlett to ask if she intended to keep the dog, she'd made noises about potentially passing him onto a breeder - who was apparently a very dear and close friend. Fortunately, Auryn was well-versed in animal dealing and had read it for what it was - she wanted money.

Out of interest, I'd done some research into Scarlett's underwear firm in the days that had followed Ethan's arrest. I'd discovered that the merger was indeed her company swallowing up a smaller competitor, and that Scarlett herself was incredibly well-off. It might have seemed greedy for someone of her wealth to ask for money for a dog she didn't want to keep, but I thought I understood. She had loved Timmy, but he'd given her the runaround. She'd paid him back in kind, but beneath all that they'd played some pretty spiteful games. Selling Rameses was just a final equaliser to match Timmy's surprising will and the shocking truth it had revealed.

When Auryn had gone to pick up all of Rameses' pedigree papers, he'd asked about Lizzie and Will Marsden. To my surprise, Scarlett had informed Auryn that the couple were still going strong. Apparently, Will had been very accepting of the decision Lizzie and Timmy had made at that relatively early time in their lives. And although it hurt him to think of his brother with his now-wife, Will had apparently acknowledged that without the relationship between Timmy and Lizzie, he might never have met her at all. For once, it seemed that true love had found a way.

"Tiff!" I said, surprised to see my friend standing on my doorstep.

"Madi!" she said in response and then giggled.

"Someone's in a good mood." I smiled at her.

"You bet I am! Look!" Tiff thrust out her left hand to show a glittering diamond ring taking pride of place on her ring finger. My stomach seemed to do several somersaults before settling somewhere down by my feet.

"Is it… Pierce?"

"No! Of course not," Tiff frowned. "Did you really think he was the one?"

"No, well… yes, maybe. But I hoped not. It just struck me as the sort of thing he might do in order to win," I explained.

Tiff's frown deepened. "But you don't think Detective Gregory would have done the same thing for the same reason?"

"Detective Gregory asked you to marry him? That's great!" I said, injecting as much enthusiasm into my voice as I could. Tiff's expression let me know I was making a mess of it.

Fortunately, my best friend knew that I only meant well, so she rolled her eyes and walked into the house.

"I know it's all a bit sudden, but when you know, you just know. Do you understand?" She looked searchingly at me.

"I do," I told her, managing a real smile this time around. "All I want is for you to be happy. I think he's a good man. I really do."

"Thank you," she said with a smile and then, thank the heavens, she breezed right on back out of the house. "I have to tell my parents. They're going to be so excited! I'm pretty sure some people will have to pay out! Because they were betting against it ever happening," she clarified.

"What? Why would anyone think that?"

She shrugged. "Some members of my family seem to think I'm some kind of man eater. Roar!" She mimed claws.

I shook my head. "It's not your fault you're amazing."

"Oh, you," Tiff said with a grin before bouncing off full of sunshine and joy.

I watched her go while my own stomach filled up with butterflies on her behalf. I wanted Tiff to be happy, I really did, but I was also very used to seeing her with a broken heart. I hoped that this incredibly hasty proposal wasn't just Detective Gregory's move to get one over my PR and marketing manager. If that's all it was, he was going to be very sorry indeed…

My phone rang before I could dwell on it anymore. The knot of worry in my stomach grew bigger when I saw Pierce's name flash up on screen. "Now what?" I muttered, answering the phone.

"It is with regret that I would like to tender my resignation," he began. "I hope you are able to find a suitable and good replacement soon, but I am unable to continue to work for you due to unforeseen personal circumstances."

"I don't suppose you mean because you lost out on Tiff?" I asked, bemused.

"It's far more complicated than that," Pierce told me airily. "Anyway, good luck!" And with that, he hung up.

I silently reflected that it was the first time Pierce hadn't managed to sell me on him being right. Typical. Now I needed to find someone at least half as talented as Pierce, or my restaurant, and perhaps even the zoo itself, could be dead in the water.

It was like being stuck in eternal torture. After the last shambles of an interview, I'd changed the criteria to describe someone a lot like Pierce. I'd even upped the salary to his initial requirements, but still the same bunch of inept and uninspiring candidates mooched through the door.

Worse than that, word must have got out that I conducted interviews personally. Some of the people who'd applied had straight up lied on their applications just so they could get an 'exclusive interview' with me. They'd been kicked out as soon as I'd smelled journalism. Right now, it was a toss up between an ex-marketing manager from a high street store, who I knew had no experience of small business marketing, and a very enthusiastic mum who had made her cat a star on Instagram.

I sighed and rested my head in my hands for a moment before pulling myself together and steeling myself for the next candidate. I glanced at the name on the list before walking to the door and opening it. "Joe Harvey, please come in," I said to the last few remaining people waiting in line.

A young man with dark hair stood up and followed me into the room. I observed that he possessed the kind of jawline other men would die for and women surely flocked to, before I shut the thought down and remembered I was conducting professional interviews. And who knew? Perhaps this one would be the one.

I'd been telling myself that for the past ten candidates.

"Please, take a seat." I gestured to the chair behind my desk. "I'm Madigan Amos, owner of The Lucky Zoo. But please feel free to call me Madi." I smiled. It was a little idea I'd thought of to break the ice and make things a little more informal. I wanted to see people at their best, and I knew that nerves often crept in during an interview situation. Having said that, the man opposite the table was watching me with an amused look that somehow reminded me of the way

Pierce had seemed to treat everything like a joke. And yet, he'd still managed to alter my opinions and, more importantly, prove his worth by bringing in people and publicity.

"How about we start with prior experience? What experience do you feel you have that makes you right for this role?" I asked, making sure to continue to smile. The amusement in the man's striking blue eyes was starting to unnerve me. Whilst he thought about the question, I cast an admiring look in the direction of his dark hair. It was longer than a conventional short back and sides, but he kept it swept back from his face, apart from a few strands that had flopped forwards, like a dark comma above his eyebrows.

"While I don't have a degree or even any qualifications in marketing or PR, I do have a fantastic track record." He flashed his white teeth at me. "If you employ me, you will see my salary come back to you several times over within a year."

I felt my ears prick up. Was this man cut from the same cloth as Pierce? He wasn't quite as devilishly smooth, but I found I was almost willing to take him up on the offer. "Would you mind letting me know more about that fantastic track record?"

"Sure! I've got a lot of experience with international companies who specialise in import and export. Perhaps more relevant to this role, I'm well-versed in marketing unique products that need to be packaged and marketed creatively. I was recently part of a team who launched a new author. She then went on to become a global success."

I lifted my head sharply, meeting the striking blue eyes of the man sat opposite me. Then I looked, I really looked at him. For a moment neither of us said anything.

"Jordan?" I said, almost as a whisper, wondering if I was going crazy. This man had a far more prominent jawline and his cheeks had been filled out, so that those cheekbones I'd once admired were no longer visible. Then there was the hair and the eyes. He'd even bulked out a lot, and I sensed there were more muscles than slenderness beneath the charcoal suit he wore. He looked like a different man.

Perhaps he was a different man.

I looked up again, wondering if my most eligible candidate was about to run out of the room shouting about the crazy woman who'd just called him by another name.

"It's Joe," he said, but his smile told a different story.

I was right. My old literary agent, who was currently wanted by MI5, was sitting across the desk from me.

The silence stretched on for a few more seconds before he leant forwards and raised his eyebrows. "So... have I got the job?"

BOOKS IN THE SERIES

Penguins and Mortal Peril

The Silence of the Snakes

Murder is a Monkey's Game

Lions and the Living Dead

The Peacock's Poison

A Memory for Murder

Whales and a Watery Grave

Chameleons and a Corpse

Foxes and Fatal Attraction

Monday's Murderer

Prequel: Parrots and Payback

A REVIEW IS WORTH ITS WEIGHT IN GOLD!

I really hope you enjoyed reading this story. I was wondering if you could spare a couple of moments to rate and review this book? As an indie author, one of the best ways you can help support my dream of being an author is to leave me a review on your favourite online book store, or even tell your friends.

Reviews help other readers, just like you, to take a chance on a new writer!

Thank you!
Ruby Loren

Made in United States
North Haven, CT
20 July 2022

21614878R00129